Dreaming Walls

Dreaming Walls

by Krzysztof Maciejewski

PAPERBACK ISBN: 978-1-7348606-7-2
EPUB ISBN: 978-1-3930908-3-0

***

WRITTEN BY KRZYSZTOF MACIEJEWSKI
PUBLISHED BY ROYAL HAWAIIAN PRESS
COVER ART BY TYRONE ROSHANTHA
TRANSLATED BY WIESLAWA MENTZEN
PUBLISHING ASSISTANCE: DOROTA RESZKE

***

FOR MORE WORKS BY THIS AUTHOR, PLEASE VISIT:
WWW.ROYALHAWAIIANPRESS.COM

***

VERSION NUMBER 1.00

Maybe all the dragons in our lives are princesses who are waiting for us to act beautifully and courageously at least once. Maybe everything that scares us, is in its deepest being something helpless, desiring our love.

JONATHAN CARROLL, A CHILD IN THE SKY

Prologue

Corpses should be viewed in blue light, it brings out the most beautiful side of them. These are the conclusions reached by the observer from the inside of the wall, who con......,....:es this unearthly view in a sudden surge of reverie.

The delicate light seems to caress the dead body, as if it were dealing with a patient afflicted with *osteogenesis imperfecta*, as if it played a glass harp or a violin, woven of rain. Maybe it is because of this inherent delicacy that it lays its azure shadows so lightly? The observer recalls the winter days of his childhood, when in sunny weather, the shaded snow reflected the blue of the sky. Or the view of the crystal waters of a lake, which hid its own nightmares and secrets somewhere in its depths.

The dead man was not a beau when alive, his face was far from the Hollywood standards. But the observer, whose eyes look from behind the wall, does not care about appearances. Besides, he too belongs to the same aesthetic category, closer to the Neanderthal than to Brad Pitt. The cadaver lies motionless at the bottom of his own lake, which is not surprising at all, it would be a lot stranger if he were pirouetting or practicing moonwalking. And yet there is an elusive appearance of life in him, one can feel an almost broken rhythm of a breath. Almost.

Because the dead has been lying here for a week already, stretched horizontally in the long empty corridor of the deserted house. The observer knows that its inhabitants will return soon, but he does not even try to guess their reaction to this unusual scenography. It's even harder to guess with what actions they will respond to everything that will happen later. In fact, he is feeling great sadness right now just thinking about it. Because the corpses look picturesque in the cobalt lighting, but in the light of the day they can be terrifying. And the dreams? What will happen to the dreams?

The witness of the dead show, with the corpse and the light in the lead roles, turns away from the blue, the lake, the snow. His eyes blink in the dark for a moment, then close. The brightness loses its color and becomes darkness again.

Chapter 1

MARC AND MARTHA

Returns are not the favorite moments of my life. We are usually stuck in a traffic jam, nervously suppressing the curses from escaping our mouths (because we are travel with the kids), but in our minds, we yell a very offensive litany of profanities. The toddlers complain, the conversation doesn't flow, time runs away into black holes like a strangelet. Hermann Hesse wasn't right when he said that one never returns home, but rather the whole world momentarily seems to be home in a place where friendly paths intersect. Apparently, the German Nobel Prize winner did not take into account the fact that the intersection of the friendly roads welcomed us by a massive traffic jam, consisting of hundreds of cars driven by pissed drivers.

We were coming back from the holidays, which once again did not take place during the holiday season. Every year we rather go in June or September to avoid the flood of humans at the resorts. In spite of this, every year we return in gigantic traffic jams.

Fortunately, Sophie and Kallen fell asleep in the backseat. Such a trip can be tiring for an adult, let alone a nine-year-old. Martha also began a nap, but after all, we have just recently changed behind the wheel so she had a good reason to feel tired. The distance to the house was shortening at a walking pace, so I sank in thoughts. Rather unhappy thoughts, I won't deny. Tomorrow, I'll have to put on the mask of a rested man and report to work in the morning. But there was something else, something lurking somewhere in the shadow of neurons and causing a strange anxiety. I blamed the exhaustion with the long journey for it. Hell, I just knew that we should have gotten up early in the morning! We would be in front of all those morons in their cars, missing their sofas.

7

Many years later I wondered how it all began. In what moment the ominous dark colors started sneaking into our fairly boring, but quiet life? Because it is so, that at a certain age you stop looking for stars, and you decide to live here and now, in the safe, albeit perhaps constrained space. That's how it was with us.

Martha worked in the financial sector, but fortunately she was not a corporation slave, so she returned home at normal hours. I've been doing various gigs and projects - you know, translations, instructions, short articles (are there any other articles than short in the Internet age?). The children went to kindergarten, then to school, like others of their age. In one word, we lived in a quiet oasis, until everything suddenly ended, and it happened during our return from the September holidays. The first harbinger of the madness was a stranger. I simply suddenly noticed a movement in the backseat of the car moving slowly in front of us. Bang! The woman, because it was probably a woman, turned toward me and stared at me persistently. Boy, was she ugly! We all remember our childhood nightmares, when the mind transforms the first tales we hear into its own images. Really terrifying faces of evil witches appear in these inner pictures, far from the sweet Disney animations, full of distorted noses, faces with fragments torn off, unearthly shapes of the eyes. It was such a dream that the passenger of the car in front of us came from. She stared at me for a moment, then turned back to the driver.

And then Martha screamed.

***

Immobility. Total paralysis. She is lying in bed, concerned faces are leaning towards her, and some faces express something like a reproach. She wants to shout, because it's not her fault that she rests in an invisible cage in the shape of her body, like a dying butterfly with a giant's pin penetrating the exoskeleton, forever combining the sky with a hard surface. It is a total incapacitation, a model presentation of the topic of enslavement, a complete dependence on the owners of these faces suddenly twitching in strange grimaces, peeling at a rapid pace, and dripping with plasma and green mucus.

And suddenly she is no longer in bed, she has found herself in a deep pit, to which curious organs of vision look, some hidden behind masks, others naked and cruelly merciless. She knows that in a moment, the rain of dirt and stones will fall on her, but even such a dangerous prospect is unable to snatch her from the state of catatonia. She can't even move her eyelids to hide in the safe world of afterimages. What she is afraid most, is not being buried alive in a moment. At some level, the most terrible thing is that in a moment the clump of earth will fall on her open eyes, which she can't close. A silent scream grows in her and then she wakes up.

***

I pulled off to the nearby parking lot, because we had to calm down the shaken kids. Of course, I could not be mad with Martha, especially since I had also just experienced a traumatic scene straight from a nightmare. Dark clouds rolled in the sky, reminiscent of conceptual shapes from Rorschach test, and my wife was telling me her dream. Our little elves calmed down enough that they got into their typical mood and began to run around the playground, near the place we parked. Martha was also calmer, but it was obvious that she was putting on a brave face.

"I mean... It was so darn realistic and so... deeply terrifying... you know," she sighed.

I hugged and kissed her.

"This road is terribly exhausting. Thanks god we're almost home," I whispered in her ear.

She returned the kiss in gratitude.

"Our beloved sweet home... There we will be able to rest."

We soon saw how far from the truth this statement was.

***

Fortunately, the way home continued without any surprises. We reached our house at Wietrzna Street before dusk, quickly plunging into the chaos of unpacking the car, children's whining, nervous shouting of the tired parents and the curious looks of the neighbors, who, of course, chose this moment for Nordic walking.

Even before we crossed the threshold of the house, we were both dead tired. Another hour passed when we unpacked the suitcases and bags, and the kids somehow did not want to help us... These are the moments in life where there is nothing cheerful, and yet with the passage of time, when you start thinking about them, you come to the conclusion that you were happy then. The screams of children can drive you mad, but you know subconsciously that these are the most beautiful sounds that can be heard in this world, the real symphonies of joy written on the musical staff of our fate. But the silence that comes from their room when they are asleep, is equally blissful...

After all this confusion, I was quietly sitting in the chair when Martha's scream came from the first floor. I quickly ran up the stairs and saw her pale face.

"Someone is lying in the corridor..." my wife said through a tight throat.

***

He did not look too pretty, so when I finally climbed the stairs and reached the corridor between the bedrooms, I quickly understood Martha's hysterical behavior. The corpse (he was definitely a corpse, because the living do not give off such odor) was dressed in bizarre rags, and his face would land him a job as an extra in the movies *Quest for fire* or *10,000 BC*.

"Well... I heard the Neanderthals did not die out, they just assimilated," I murmured.

Martha looked at me with barely restrained rage.

"We have a dead guy at home, and you feel like cracking jokes!"

"Oh, honey... I just wanted to lighten the atmosphere... You see how ugly he is?"

"I think he's a hobo," she nodded. It was evident that she was trying hard to rationalize the entire event. "He probably moved in during our absence..."

I know that I am quoting this dialogue quite freely, that it may sound a bit cinematic in your ears. But all later events put a shadow on the earlier ones, distort the perspective, change the contours of the objects and give a different meaning to what seemed obvious.

"We have to call the police," I said.

And that's what we did.

***

Two policemen in plain clothes flashed their steel badges. The shorter one had short blond hair and glasses. His bigger colleague looked like a gym lover. Just a typical intellectual of the no-neck type. The Four-Eyes smiled at us rather stiffly.

"Assistant Commissioner Dariusz Śmigielski, good evening..."

The meathead only murmured something under his breath. We invited both inside. Leading them up the stairs, for the first time I had a strange impression that someone was watching me. It was as if the wall had eyes.

Śmigielski whispered something to the muscleman, who answered in a sharp tone. Martha rolled her eyes. The shorter officer smiled apologetically at us.

"I suggested to the boss that we should wait for the technicians team. But he said that we must confirm the complaint first..."

"Boss?" I stammered.

Now they both twisted their faces in a strange grimace.

"Commissioner Sabol is a real scare for criminals," Śmigielski explained.

I looked at the big policeman and thought to myself that it is probably not only criminals who fear him. And then I turned on the light in the corridor. The cadaver was gone.

"Well, where is this tramp?" Sabol hissed.

I shook my head.

"I don't understand... Martha... He was lying here and stinking..."

But the sickly smell was gone without a trace, too. The officers shook their heads.

"Calling the police without justification is an offense under article 66..." Śmigielski said slowly.

"Commissioner..." Martha interjected. "This is not a stupid joke... We came back from our vacation and found a corpse in our house!"

"And the said corpse subsequently disappeared into thin air," Finished Śmigielski.

We could only nod in confirmation. On their way out, the police only said that they would not go after our unjustified call this time. They might consider it never happened, but we should have a good sleep, because apparently we were so tired we started seeing things. Our good byes were rather cold. When the door closed behind them, I looked at my wife.

"I think they were right... I'm exhausted."

Martha shrugged.

"OK, let's go get some sleep."

But the sleep did not bring us the desired peace.

***

The observer realizes that he made it in the very last moment. And only this matters, forget about the alternative threads in which the policemen discover the dead body in the blue glow, you can put them all away on the shelf. The Mystery of the Harpists remains unthreatened, but the terrifying fate of the residents of the house does not let the observer sleep for a long time. But the sleep will finally come, it always does - even if we are too tired to take it under our roof. Even if the shadows extend beyond the range of light, making the darkness itself drip with the dark. Even then.

Chapter 2

MARTHA

I will tell you about the deathlings*... When I was a little girl, I played with other children by the pond near the old house of my grandparents. We used to go there often in these old day which at times seem to change into mythical tales from celluloid and yellowed pages. A small waterfall fell from the rock steps, and we often threw stones or other objects towards it. I liked best to throw an old bone, which had to belong to a cow in its previous incarnation. One day the bone disappeared. I searched for it frantically by the water, where it always fell, but it was as if a devil covered it with his tail. I was growing up....

Deathlings are sharp-edged objects that smooth down over time, hide their spines, dull their beaks. Adults do not see them, because their eyes are used to predetermined shapes, to filling the space according to a pattern. When we grow up, the deathlings are absorbed by the smooth surfaces, which the adult eye can see. Adults do not want to see deathlings, just as they do not see death in its simplest form. They claim that they got comfortable with some topic, but they only lost their ability to see things. The old bone was my deathling, the old bone was my Death.

And now I thought to myself that the dead body from the corridor was also a deathling.

***

Even before going to bed, I went to the room of the kids, who slept soundly and peacefully, unaware of the events. The peace written on their faces infected me too. Of course, it was difficult to

---

* kind of a diminutive from 'death', the world does not exist in Polish

remove the picture of a dead man from my mind, or maybe it was even worse to realize that his presence somehow defiled the sacrum of our household. It's a bit difficult to defend this feeling, I know. I do not want to say that our apartment was previously unscathed by evil, and now it has been tainted. It seems that every house hides a mystery that evokes both the feeling of shame and the thrill in its owner. And yet this man was under our roof, he might have been using drugs or binge drinking. Well, I know the life of the hobos mainly from police chronicles, but somehow I do not believe it is idyllic. Well, you know, like in John Steinbeck's Tortilla Flat. If we stick to Steinbeck, then the Grapes of Wrath speak to me more.

However, I did not have the luxury to think about my favorite readings any longer. I had to be at work the next day, so I calmly prepared everything I would need. I am a manager in a small financial consulting company - it is a very distant world from holiday walks on beach at dusk and the disappearing sounds of a day.

I returned to Marc, but my husband was also asleep already. It would be futile to look for relief and bliss on his face. The poor man was probably having a nightmare. I sighed quietly and turned off the bedside lamp, sensing that my dreams would also be nothing like the fairy-tale lands, filled with singing and Disney-like colors. I turned and tossed for a very long time, trying to get in an optimal position in which I would find a child's carefree attitude. And then I remembered that supposedly only the madmen have colorful dreams.

***

Behind the Peninsula of Anxiety, a small town of girls appears. There is an eternal silence in it, because its inhabitants never make any sound. There is a silent wind blowing along the streets of the town, and the silent sea crashes against monotonously gray stones at its coast. Dead beaches surround a long-deserted port, where old sailing ships are dying, condemned to going to sleep. Even the colors have been banished and all streets are uniformly monochrome. This, however, does not bother the girls living here. Residents of the city behind the Peninsula of Anxiety in the right Hemisphere disseminate thoughts. I know it well, I'm wandering in this old movie displayed under the head's dome. I am just an observer, I am not one of them - the awareness of this alienation causes fear that is difficult to describe.

Thoughts resemble floral bouquets with their shape. But - just like everything else in the town - they were stripped of colors. It is only the mind of the Thinker who dresses them in the right colors. The stewardesses of thoughts do not mind the dead gray. What is important is that the load does not weigh too much and that it is delivered to the destination on time. Even the most memorable reflections are light - maybe so that the little girls could carry them. Sometimes, however, they are so extensive that they have to be moved in special baskets. Then the stewardesses quietly complain about their fate, but nobody ever hears them anyway. Even I, dreaming this dream somewhere on the verge of horror, I can't hear their whispers.

Where do thoughts come from? It is said that black swans bring them at night. However, after some time, thoughts have to leave the town. If it is not clearly specified, they end up in a dump behind the peninsula, where they die. A meaningless thought is dead anyway. Other type of thought must be transported to the wasteland, adjacent to the town on the west. Such an expedition can be quite boring. Thoughts left in the wasteland mature with time and change shape. Sometimes they return to the seaside town, from where they can be sent to the dumps or to the Abyss.

To get to the Abyss, you have to put on your wings first. With wings on their back, the faded girls resemble angels from rural church carnivals. However, the wings are not just a decorative motif

- they are used as a means of transport. The abyss stretches far beyond the horizon. Whoever wants to get there, must prepare not only for a long flight over the whispering desert, but also to face the mystery. None of the girls sent with a bouquet of thoughts to the Abyss ever returned. There are thoughts that must be destroyed, which must be thrown into the Abyss, before they cause more damage. Someone must be sacrificed then - even if it means a small girl, unnecessary for anyone.

And I am flying following them, I know that I will not be able to return to the quiet alleys of the town. The Abyss attracts me, grinning its toothy jaws, calls me with a low wheeze, which starts to rattle in my chest. Suddenly, the winged girls turn to face me, and their faces melt like wax. The dead skulls, dripping with mucus, smile at me as I start screaming...

* * *

Marc, who apparently woke up from his own horror, also screams. We look at each other for a moment, then we cuddle. I report the content of the dream to him, quickly and chaotically, and he does the same. Two deadly scared people sharing the terrifying stories to make one another feel better. But that's how love works, in case you did not know...

Marc dreamed of a deep well, in which he was falling (yes, I noticed the resemblance to the Abyss!). The worst thing was not the feeling of a free fall in anticipation of hitting the surface of the water, but the algae creatures touching him during his flight, and whispering something in a long-forgotten language.

Marc thinks something is happening that goes beyond our understanding. These dreams and the mysterious corpse, dematerializing after the arrival of police officers, must have something in common.

* * *

"We do not understand it, at least for now, but in the end everything will be clear," said Marc, looking at me searchingly. I love this gaze, remembering very well what impression it makes on his interlocutors. Especially those who try to hide some of their shady activities. My beloved husband in one of his many incarnations as a political journalist on one of the online portals!

"We must protect Sophie and Kallen at all costs," I said. OK, dreams, politics, all fine but the kids are most important. I was surprised myself that I was so calm.

"That's exactly why we have to strive to solve the mystery." Marc's reporter's instinct sometimes won even with his concern for the family. Sometimes it scared me.

"Take care of it then. You know, the politicians and the disintegrating Neanderthals are probably not too far from each other," I replied sneeringly.

Marc got somewhat disconcerted for a moment. But the flash in his eyes did not dim.

"Well... So, the theory number one..," It's fatigue, and the corpse in our hall was just a dream. It was just another one of the nightmares that have tormented us for some time.

Should I have explained to him then that the prehistoric deceased was not an embodied dream, but a deathling? I did not do it, because I never shared that childhood memory with him. Was it a lack of honesty? No, rather a retreat to a secret garden that occupies a small corner in every woman's soul. Guys have their caves, and we cultivate colorful flowers on the flower beds of our souls. As the old man Boss sings, a man may be close to a girl, but her secret garden is always thousands of miles from the male heart.

"I mean, you know... Why do you assume that these events are connected?" I asked, raising my eyebrows slightly.

"It's elementary, dear Watson..," he began. "But I do not know yet. I just have this feeling."

"And do you have a feeling of what we should do now?"

Alright, it was a bit stinging on my part. But malice is a characteristics of intelligent people, and I knew that my husband also values me for my intellect.

"My inner self tells me that we should get some sleep..."

"Aren't you afraid of monsters lurking under your eyelids?" I smiled at him.

He returned the smile.

"I am so exhausted that I will not even notice them..."

And that's what actually happened. Maybe we've exhausted the daily (or actually the nightly) limit of horror? The following days showed however, that bankers from the Bank of Fears raise all possible limits of horror for us. After only a week, I could only hope we would not accumulate debt...

**

And what are the Harpists doing at this time? A trivial puzzle. They are playing harps, of course. And they sound amazingly melodious. It is a pity that no one will appreciate this performance, no one will hear a single sound filling the concert hall hidden in the wall.

SOMEONE ELSE IS DREAMING I

I fell asleep, but now I do not know if I was a detective or his assistant in the dream... Or maybe I became each of them, I penetrated both minds, I remembered as much as I could. It was like this.

I have always believed in the existence of invisible patterns, according to which life goes on. I remember how one day I told Dermott that we were only repeating the patterns of other people's behaviors, like passive puppets or silhouettes dancing on the wall in some ghostly shadow theater. He then looked at me with indulgence. "We are something more, my friend. Gray cells, supported by the ability to analyze and observe, give us power over the world," he replied with emphasis. But it was a long time ago, even before the mystery of the twin cities, which was the crowning achievement, and at the same time the last episode of the career of Dermott de Valois, the greatest detective of all time. Well, finis coronat opus...

I will emphasize here that the quoted opinion is only my own judgment and verdict, because, although it would be difficult to call my friend overly modest,, he did not like - these are his words - to compete with shadows. I once asked him about his opinion on the various famous detectives of the past. Dermott was silent for a moment, then a strange expression appeared on his face.

"You mean the fictional creations of the imagination of various writers?" He asked.

When I nodded to confirm, his eyes were dimmed by a shadow of disapproval.

"Well... Let's take a Mr. Dupin, who dazzles his interlocutors with cheap tricks, as Holmes rightly pointed out to him... He had too much of his sullen and desperate protoplast in him to really represent something of his own. Next... Hercule Poirot, a funny figure who uses a dagger-sharp analysis, but often does not see quite obvious relations. And how long does it take him to get to the truth... It's partly a fault of the convention in which Mrs. Christie wrote her books... Not to mention that some of her stories are at odds with logic..."

"Well, and the aforementioned Sherlock Holmes?" I interrupted him.

Dermott pursed his lips.

"He, in turn, did not notice certain nuances, he paid almost no attention to emotions, reminding a hound following a scent. But do you know what is the main complaint I must make about my predecessors?"

-"They were unrealistic?" I took a chance.

Dermott winced, indignant.

"I do not mean such obvious clichés, dear Harrison. I mean their shortcomings in being well read... None of them has studied literature, which opens our eyes to many things, and above all, it provides a lot of material on human reactions. How could they then learn the personality of the murderer if they did not know the mentality of ordinary people?"

"And Miss Marple?" I asked. "She used this analogy method..."

"But, my friend... The old woman referred to the inhabitants of her village, as if she could find all patterns of behavior there. Do you really believe in this microcosm, limited to a few dozens of houses, because this idea seems a bit of a stretch to me? It is another story if you delve into a variety of fictitious worlds, you enter a lot of roles, traversing the depths of time and space in the flight of soaring shoals of stars... You just have to read between the lines."

Dermott's point of view was not just a mere doctrine. He caught a murderer once, who left a printed letter at the crime scene. On the basis of some mysterious premises, he was able to recognize the author of the message, quickly fishing him out of the circle of suspects. Still another time, at the very beginning of our acquaintance, he left me utterly amazed. We were sitting there that morning, busy reading newspapers and our mail as usual. Suddenly I spoke to Dermott, very amused by one of the statements of my cousin, who described her last shopping dilemmas - going into details a bit excessively, in my opinion:

"Imagine that Ginny can't decide which phone model suits her personality best..."

But Dermott interrupted me in a rather abrupt way:

"Harrison, it's the confidentiality of the mail! You should not share such confessions with an almost stranger!"

I looked at him, slightly baffled.

"What are you talking about? After all, it is just an ordinary letter talking about very trivial matters..."

My friend shrugged.

"I can tell you a lot about your cousin based on a few sentences she wrote..."

"Are you also a graphologist, Dermott? I'm going to disappoint you, but Ginny never sends handwritten letters. You will not learn anything..."

Dermott laughed loudly. His laughter was not joyful though.

"Since you say that there are no dark secrets in the letter, give it to me to read. And then you will listen to the conclusions I'll have reached from the reading."

I must admit that in the beginnings of our acquaintance, the detective was getting on my nerves quite a lot. I decided that it was a great opportunity to take him down a peg. I handed the letter to him with a slight smile, and Dermott started reading. After ten minutes, he lit a pipe and looked at me, sparks dancing wildly in his eyes.

"Well... Your cousin is a few years younger than you, she has blond hair now, although a few months ago its color was probably quite different. Her eyes are certainly dark, although I do not see their color exactly. She is quite a small woman, but with a strong character. She loves animals, but she does not have dogs or cats at home. She is probably an artistic soul, and science was not her forte in school. Oh... And in two minutes she'll be at the door..." he looked at me triumphantly.

"This... this is some charlatanry," I stammered. Everything was actually correct in Dermott's description. "Where the hell did you read it all?"

"Between the lines, my friend. Between the lines," he replied in a light tone.

"But it must be a magic or something! How do you know she does not keep dogs or cats?"

Dermott smiled slightly.

"A well trained art of observation resembles a herd of horses, running along the seashore - he replied. - I come to certain conclusions, not knowing myself how or when. But in this case, it is actually easy to draw a similar hypothesis, because we are dealing with a lady with allergy... She wrote to you that she sneezed when choosing perfumes, right?"

-"Okay, but this inference seems too far-reaching..."

"I know. That's why I tried to verify this fact in the remaining part of the letter. That paragraph about a flying bee that frightened her so much confirmed the initial assumptions."

I shrugged.

"Alright, I give it to you... You guessed it right. But how do you know that she will come here in a moment?"

"Because she is standing in front of the entrance to the building... It's her, right?"

Indeed - I recognized the face of my cousin on the control screen. Much later, after she left, I tried to persuade Dermott to make further confessions. How the hell did he guess that the woman in front of the building was Ginny? But my friend shrugged me off. I suspect that it was a guess fortified with intuition, pure gambling, supported however by a colonnade of premises that for me were completely useless trinkets. Well, I was slowly getting into Dr. Watson's skin.

***

The last case of Dermott de Valois began on a gloomy day, which perched in wait behind the window like a gray-furred beast. We were called to the crime scene before ten o'clock. The victim was a thirty-year-old star of the bar, probably the youngest partner in the history of one of the most respected law firms. We drove in almost complete silence, listening to the whispers of radio specters. The city was a black and white cartoon thrown on both sides of the street, as if the rain had stripped trees and buildings of their proper colors.

The house in which the bloody murder was carried out, was a perfect example of the bad taste that characterized young professionals, the chewers on the meal served by TV, at whom the fate smiled. Golden decorations on the chimney, festoons of artificial flowers hanging above the windows - in a word - a pathetic plastic pretending to be eclectic.

"Perhaps the murderer was sent by the architecture department?" I said quietly to Dermott, but my friend did not react.

We entered the first floor, escorted by two young constables. At the top of the stairs stood concerned inspector Hill-Burton. His face brightened at our sight. He greeted me, then turned to Dermott, completely ignoring my humble person.

"I'm glad you are here. I do not know what to think about all this."

De Valois was a policeman once, but he retreated to an early retirement. Now, however, he often played the role of a consultant.

We went into the room where the victim had been found. The man lay in the middle of the floor in a pool of blood, reminding a great dead bird shot down from the sky.

"What have you discovered?" Dermott said to Hill-Burton.

"The crime took place about five hours ago, around six in the morning. The man was stabbed about a dozen times with a sharp tool, but we do not know what it was. There is no evidence. Nobody heard anything."

So we probably could not count on witnesses. Dermott looked around the room and after a moment his eyes fell on the front door.

"Was there a break-in?"

Hill-Burton blinked nervously.

"This is the strangest thing in all this. The door was bolted from the inside. We had to use a crowbar to get inside."

"Interesting..." Murmured my friend. "Can I have a look around?"

"Make yourself at home," the policeman replied quickly, realizing after a moment the impropriety of these words.

Dermott, however, did not pay any attention to the clearly confused inspector. He watched the dead man's body carefully, his face becoming more and more worried with each passing minute. He spent a lot of time checking the room. He stared for a long moment at the mirror hanging on the wall, as if searching in it for answers to the questions that were tormenting him. When he finished the inspection, he returned to us, but no emotion could be read from his face.

"Do you have something, Dermott?" I asked.

"Nothing at all. The murderer did not leave any trace or fingerprint... Let's interrogate whoever we can..."

My friend was clearly worried. While we were coming back, at some point he turned to me.

"Did you notice the sterile order in the room, Harrison? Not even the slightest hint. It's even weirder than the whole story with the closed door..."

"Why do you think so?"

My friend was silent for a moment, trying to translate his galloping thoughts into a spoken language.

"As if the murder was committed in a completely different place. Damn it! I even feel like the victim was in fact a completely different person. But it is impossible..."

I would soon remember these words in very strange circumstances.

* * *

No, we did not keep in touch at all. You understand, Morten was not too effusive. I suspect he did not have friends or enemies.

I think that only work was important to him. He breathed it, he endured all inconveniences for it. Relatives? He did not need people. He was a caveman, he liked being alone.

Morten's enemies? Lawyers create a small world. Pardon? Well, of course, we compete with each other on professional basis. He was a legal adviser to many well-known corporations, but no one envied him that. Competition on the market? Do you believe in the conspiracy theory of the functioning of a free economy? In mysterious industrial spies, carrying out trade secrets on microfilms? It's possible, but lawyers are outside the system. Believe me...

Women? Well, he certainly was not a monk, but he wasn't in a stable relationship with anyone. You know the saying: "if you want to drink a beer, you don't have to buy the majority share in a brewery"? No, I do not think he hurts these women. They agreed on everything, they were aware of the roles that the convention set for them... No, he wasn't that close to anyone.

He took a vacation. Yes, the first one in four years. Nobody saw him. We thought that he wanted to be left alone.

What can I tell you, Dermott? You saw the body... I don't know which one of the wounds was fatal. Pardon? A peculiar pattern of the wounds that resembles a Chinese ideogram? You must be kidding! It's a pure coincidence, my friend. In the clouds, we also sometimes recognize different outlines, but this is just a childishness. No, my dear. Fate is settled in the stars, not in the clouds.

***

Dermott was getting more and more unbearable every day. I knew that the investigation was not bringing the desired results, and the interrogations of witnesses were leading nowhere, which had to humiliate my friend like a glove thrown in his face. Finally, when he decided that the traditional intelligence methods had failed, he sat at the console and launched a special portal connecting him with the Spider Specter Web.

Even for people who were well versed in technology, it was witchcraft. Dermott tried to explain to me the principle of the spectral network once. I did not understand much of these explanations. I only know that the Spider Specter Web was some kind of ultimate reflection of the virtual world of the Internet. I imagined it as underground tunnels hollowed out under busy paths, or maybe as shadows of ordinary Internet connections, hidden from the eyes of outsiders. Dermott believed that the classic web turned into a heap of garbage, where it is very difficult to find anything valuable. In his opinion, the Spider Specter Web still had the pristine character that the spaces woven from conventional connections had lost long ago.

So my friend sat down at the console and activated his own tracking program, created in ancient times, to which he did not like to come back in his memories. After about half an hour, he got up, and a strange expression appeared on his face.

"Did you find something, my friend?" I asked curiously.

"I don't know yet..." he replied. "In any case, we're going to Aachen."

***

At first, the German police officer was very wary about our explanations, which was hardly surprising. However, when Dermott showed the letters of recommendation from Scotland Yard, the situation changed like the fate of the oppressed workers after the revolution in Soviet propaganda films. The archives were quickly made available to us, and Dermott could exchange a few words with the investigating officer.

"So the murder took place at eight o'clock, that is six o'clock in Greenwich Mean Time?"

"That's right, Mr. de Valois."

"The room was bolted from the inside, and the victim was lying on the floor, stubbed a dozen times with a sharp tool that was not found?" Dermott demanded.

"That's correct…"

"Did the wounds on the victim's body form any pattern?"

"I'm afraid I don't understand…"

-"Can I see the pictures of the murdered?"

"Of course."

I stared at my friend's face, decorated with a smile that was getting wider and wider. A moment later, the German officer returned with a briefcase under his arm. Dermott snatched it away from him in an abrupt gesture. He took out photographs from inside and selected one of them. After a while he threw his arms up triumphantly.

"I knew it!" He shouted.

"What's going on, Dermott?" I asked, slightly worried by the behavior of my friend, who rarely let himself be carried away by emotions.

"Look, Harrison, at this picture…" his face was beaming. "The wounds form the same shape we saw on the body in London."

"But… What does this mean?"

"How come, Harrison, you don't know? This is obviously a Chinese ideogram, which we usually translate as 'the same' or 'twin'!"

I was still confused.

"Dermott… I do not understand… Who is the murderer then?"

My friend looked at me with a clear disapproval in his eyes.

"Oh, my dear. I don't know yet. However, I discovered a pattern, a matrix of connections! It will be downhill from here!"

I did not share Dermott's optimism. It's weird, but it just occurred to me that it was the first time I was right.

***

Soon Dermott became depressed. He spent all day at the console, consulted the spider specters, but even they could not get him out of this state. I had some satisfaction, because I remembered well, as many months before, Dermott insisted that all he needed to do was to ask the digital ghosts the right question, and all doubts would dissolve in the mist. However, my friend's suffering became more and more visible, he lost his appetite and I immediately felt ashamed that I was guided by such low motives.

One day Dermott rolled out of his office. The blue circles under his eyes looked like wild flowers.

"You got something?" I asked the question, trying very hard to make my voice sound cordial.

"Oh, Harrison... It's just a hypothesis... I have to verify it, because I will not talk about such heresies until I make sure they're true."

It was unlike him. He usually did not care about the opinions of others, and sometimes he articulated even just vague assumptions.

"How long will it take you to check your theory?" I asked him carefully.

"In the evening we will put everything to attention," he drawled.

There were furrows plowed under his eyes, and his face resembled an immobile mask. I knew that Dermott already knew the answer to the question tormenting him, and that he did not like it at all.

***

From the journal of Dermott de Valois:

In the childhood world, populated by monsters, a mirror has its own special place. Apart from the terrifying creatures living in wardrobes, and beasts sleeping under the bed, there is a definite ban on looking in the mirror between midnight and dawn. According to Chinese legends, the sinister Ngum-Pao live in the night mirrors, devouring the insomnia-suffering souls of those affected by narcissism. Jewish tales, in turn, evoke the figure of a mysterious *demon with a thousand faces, whom we will see if we carelessly approach a mirror at night. Also in Arab homes there was a centuries-old custom to cover silver-plated glass at dusk. But there are also cultures that reject mirrors in their entirety, treating them as suspiciously as iconoclasts treat the cult of images. Are all these premises any clue to me? Have there been twin murders hundreds of or even thousands of years ago? Can I believe in such far-fetched theories, suggested to me by digital ghosts?*

So I had to deal with the fears older than a rational attitude denying the existence of mirror ghosts. Anyway, the recent events have definitely put me in a metaphysical mood. I decided to follow the trail of the murderer from the mirrors.

A protagonist of Gothic horror novels would walk down a long hallway, illuminated by flickering candle flames, and at the very end of the hallway he would see a mirror. I went to the bathroom in the dark, hitting my elbow painfully on the door frame. I did not turn on the light so as not to scare away any shadow. Standing in front of the sink, I put my hand in my pocket and took out a lighter. Illuminating my physiognomy with a dim light, I looked at the mirror and saw in it a murderer...

***

I was sitting in the light of the lamp, and holding pictures in my hands. Dermott had printed them a moment ago.

"What's in them?"

"You tell me, Harrison. What do you see? "

The photo prints showed dead bodies, marked with a bloody alphabet of wounds. I noticed that each of the photos was repeated in duplicate.

"Why double copies, Dermott?"

The detective looked at me with a strange smile.

30

"*These are not copies... Do you remember the Aachen corpse, stabbed in the same way as our lawyer? There was also an identical pattern of stab wounds there. You see, Harrison... You have thirteen similar, double sets in front of you. The murders were carried out in places far from each other, in the same way, at the same time...*"

I looked suspiciously at my friend.

"*It must be impossible?*"

"*And yet...*"

"*But... What does this actually prove? What is your theory?*"

Dermott sighed.

"*It will be difficult for you to believe it. However, the emerging pattern is completely unambiguous. Imagine that cities have their counterparts, mirror reflections. New York may be the reflection of Lübeck, Kuala Lumpur - Boston, and London - Aachen. But on the other hand, the reflection of Paris may be a small village in Slovakia, do you understand? Size does not matter.*"

"*Size does not matter,*" *I repeated mechanically.*

"*I simply concluded that every crime committed in one of the twin cities, as I called them, has its counterpart in the corresponding place on the other side of the mirror. And then there is no point in looking for the guilty...*"

"*But, Dermott...*" *I interrupted him.* "*It really sounds like a heresy...*"

"*I verified it, Harrison... I showed you only a dozen examples of the printouts... Spectral spiders have found several hundred other killings confirming this rule.*"

I was silent for a moment.

"*Does it mean that our lawyer was killed by some drug addict from Aachen with the help of a mirror?*"

"*No. The killer is simply a mirror,*" *Dermott replied and locked himself in his room.*

***

From the diary of Dermott de Valois:

Illuminating my physiognomy with a dim light, I looked in the mirror and saw the murderer in it. It did not surprise me at all that he looked just like me. At least at the first glance. Because after a short while, the impression of identity fled somewhere among the mirror shadows. Because I realized in a sudden epiphany, that although the mirror killer looked like my twin brother, with the principle of reversing the sides of the world, it was not my reflection at all. My own eyes looked at me in a way I had never looked before. And this flash of understanding that burned in them was not at all the effect of thought processes in my brain, but rather some cruel joke. Because my face looked like a mask stripped of my own skull, and yet I could sense that it was capable of the facial expressions that I could not even imagine. And then the figure in the mirror turned his back on me and left. And I understood that I would only solve all the secrets by following his footsteps...

***

When Dermott finally left the room, he smiled at me. I looked at him uncertainly.

"I have a puzzle for you, dear Harrison," he said. "What will we see in two mirrors brought to face each other?"

I was not sure if my friend had completely lost his mind, or if the fatigue got to him.

"I do not know, Dermott," I replied in a weak voice.

"A gate, my friend," De Valois exclaimed triumphantly.

***

From the diary of Dermott de Valois:

Creating a mirror portal was fabulously simple. In the old days, when mirrors symbolized nothing but vanity, and I didn't take such curiosities quite seriously, I received the exact instructions for its construction from spectral spiders. Two mirrors reflecting in one another symbolized infinity, but at some point the image shift caused a rapture of photons, and by looking at the right angle, one was supposed to see the gate. And so it happened now, when it turned out that spectral spiders were telling the truth. Entering the mirror world, I thought for a moment that maybe I would encounter right-handed neutrinos somewhere in my way, but this thought soon dissolved in a glare. I just hoped there were no strangelets there.

***

It was a terrifying experience. Very worried about the Dermott's absence, I broke one of the rules and went into his room, of course after knocking. Unfortunately, my friend's office was empty. Only two large mirrors in the middle of the room looked for a brief moment like a deformed figure stopped in a time-lapse image. Where was Dermott? Soon I was to get an amazing answer to this question.

***

From the diary of Dermott de Valois:

I walked the strange street of the mirror city. It reminded me ideally of the places I know very well, yet it put a distorting filter on the images from the memory, a mask that we first try to ignore like a mirage displayed under our eyelids, but after a while we are no longer able to see anything else. I turned into a small street hidden in the arcades of the balconies, and I saw the murderer again. And then a rather strange reflection came to me. We are talking about someone to be a mirror image, and yet this type of rhetorical figure should rather be used to show perfect, symmetrical opposites. Does this antonym translate into a psyche, into personality traits? What I meant was that in the mirror we see our perfect opposite. So if we are good, then that figure on the other side must be perfectly evil, if we feel joy, then that other person feels sadness, and so on. The most *fascinating here is the contrast between good and evil. Who did Mother Teresa of Calcutta see in the mirror? And that's when I understood what is our darkest fear, the eternal horror. We are most afraid of these monsters that are similar to us. As if we sensed that they are the only ones who can see through our masks, ridicule each camouflage we wear confidently.*

The other Dermott looked at me with a strange smile. "You have solved the riddle of twin cities," he said. "Not quite," I replied.

***

"What is it you don't know?" I was surprised.

"I don't know where the geographical relation comes from," I replied. "I can understand that the mirror image is not only a mirror reflection, because here I have the best proof that it sometimes becomes something more. But wouldn't it be easier if you came out of mirrors and killed people in one place? Why this symmetry? Why does the murder need to have a matching crime in another, twin city?"

I looked at myself with slight indulgence.

"For pure elegance, but also for economics. If we have the opportunity to do the same thing in two different places simultaneously, why not use it?"

"Bilocation?"

"Eh... Why bilocation... What next, stigmas and miracles? Why use such a sophisticated vocabulary, such grandiloquent definitions? It's a simple trick with the mirror - every magician knows these tricks."

"Abracadabra, hocus-pocus."

"Indeed," I answered my very stressed reflection. I must admit that I watched the impression my words exerted on him with great satisfaction. And of course I could not wait to see his reaction to what

I would reveal to him in a minute. Abracadabra, hocus-pocus. It happens.

"For sure there must be a way to stop you. To stop all of you!" I exclaimed, and he again grimaced his face in a smile that did not bode well at all.

"Of course there is," I replied. "You must break all the mirrors in the world. But even if you had such an option, you would not do it."

"What would stop me?" I asked carefully.

"No motivation. Haven't you wondered even for a moment what price the mirror sets for passing through to its other side?"

I watched myself with great interest, feeling that in a moment I would know the solution to this puzzle, that in a moment my reflection would crack this puzzle with horror. I looked at myself and became more and more myself and less and less him.

"There is no hidden fee. Spiders would not lie to me on such an important issue!"

I look straight into my eyes, but I do not see the answer in them. Oh, if only I could see what my reflection was seeing with my eyes!

"Assume that you have a twin brother who just looks in the mirror and sees you. Of course, he would see a perfectly symmetrical reflection, a complete reverse."

"I don't understand..."

"Passing through the glass barrier, you have thrown away your identity. You are becoming more and more me, a ruthless murderer, and you have no chance to return anymore."

I realized that I was right because what I heard from my mouth sounded very true.

"Welcome to the Mirror People, Dermott," I said, and I heard my own sigh in response.

I sighed, and Dermott, who was me, added.

***

"You have a task to do," I hear a voice strikingly similar to mine. I open my eyes and I find myself standing in front of the bathroom mirror. When I close my eyelids, a long list appears before me, very clearly, like letters in a children's book. This is a list of people to be removed. I feel a light prick in my heart when I notice familiar names on it, but I do not really pay much attention to them. I will strike like a falcon from the sky, and then disappear in the glass surface, leaving no traces. I was a great detective, and I will become the most famous criminal in history. But first I have to leave this city.

***

This was the last case of Dermott de Valois. He probably decided that his work had lost its meaning. He soon left London and we never heard from him. Even I - his closest friend - did not know his address. I tried to find him through the Spider Specter Web, but as expected, my efforts came to naught. I returned to my private practice, I have an office in the suburbs in which I see dogs and cats, a small flat, and an eye on a young lady, for whose hand I made some efforts. I do not return to those events with my thoughts too often. Recently, however, I realized that Dermott did not take into account some of the positive aspects of this strange phenomenon. Perhaps the mirrors reflect not only crimes and rapes? Maybe it is not only murders, but also good deeds that have their counterparts in the twin cities? Just think how much hope there is in such a scenario... You fall in love with a beautiful stranger in Boston for example, and at the same time a feeling erupts between two street musicians in Kuala Lumpur... Why did not Dermott see that?

But then I imagined how my friend contorting his face contemptuously. "Love can't be put on the same scale as a murder committed in cold blood. Don't you see the difference?" He would surely say.

I often look through a newspaper, appalled by the high percentage of unexplained murders in our city. And then I remember of the conversation we had a long time ago, when the world was not divided by mirrors yet. Dermott uttered a fairly unambiguous opinion then.

"A perfect crime, Harrison? If I had to commit it, I would never be caught."

Is that why you disappeared, my friend? Please, give me a sign that you are alive and that you have not become a criminal!

***

The body of Dr. John Harrison was found at dawn on the banks of the Thames. There was a shard of a mirror in his clenched hand. It was just a small fragment of a larger whole, but it reflected the bridge and the distant quay on the other side of the river. And maybe even something more...

Chapter 3

MARC

The following days passed in a strange whirl of horrifying scenes that were suddenly shown to us during the screenings in the dream cinema. Was it then already that the ꜱ began to affect the real world, to mix with the reality? No, this stage was yet to come.

One day we were called for interrogation. It surprised us a lot, considering that the policemen did not accept our complaint after all. It turned out, however, that the disappearing deceased might be an element of a completely different case that the law enforcement agencies were occupied with. The familiar officers greeted us in the building. There was an imperceptible change in their behavior. When we sat down in a designated room, everything became clear. This time it was the Commissioner Sabol in the lead role - he sent us a wide smile, strangely mismatched with the physiognomy of a muscleman. Śmigielski was silent, he hardly looked at us, as if some internal trauma was bothering him.

"We did talk to your neighbors, no?" Sabol asked lightly. "None of them noticed any suspicious individuals loitering near the house during your absence..."

"Yes. This district does not enjoy much interest among the homeless," Śmigielski remarked dryly.

We thought we could hear a slightly contemptuous tone in his voice. "Even the homeless don't want to live there," the policeman's face suggested.

"Of course, it's harder to find a crack den or similar attractions on the outskirts of the city, no?" Added Sabol. "In any case, we must consider the case closed."

We had nothing to add. But Marc decided to investigate the strange behavior of both officers.

"Previously you did not say anything at all, Officer," he addressed the bodybuilder in uniform. "Your colleague was more talkative. And today it is the other way around... Is this some version of the good cop, bad cop strategy?"

Sabol twisted his muscleman face into a friendly grimace.

"To tell you the truth, we are not policemen by choice. We met at the acting school, no? We had the roles of a pair of, as we are called, cops, in the theater production, and we just did not manage to free ourselves from this role..."

"Now we practice the roles of different characters out of sentiment. Work is not everything, you know..." We left the place quite stunned...

**

We decided that we would both write down our dreams. We are guided in life by rather rational principles, we reject all the esoteric heritage of Egyptian dream books, horoscopes, astral bodies and haunted houses. Whenever we browse authentic Egyptian dream books, we have a lot of fun reading the entries at random. Did the ancient inhabitants of the land of pharaohs really dream about cars or rockets? We can only feel sorry for them, looking at them through the depths of time. Never mind. However, sometimes you have to make compromises with this thwarted, magical part of our reality, or maybe personality? Perhaps a dream about a fire or a deep well does not mean a good news or an influx of money, and the nightmare about a possessed town is only an emanation of the stress that torments us. Maybe, after all, it is us trying to tell ourselves something? Who knows, maybe our subconscious self sends us encrypted messages? That is why we decided to diligently record our dreams right after waking up.

***

We were in Łeba - it was high season, the beach packed so densely it could make happy only the sleazy rubbers, there was a buzz as in a school club, even though the majority of the vacationers were adult. Martha heard from someone about an empty beach in the nearby bay. We decide that we would go to look for it after lunch. I remember that I did not believe the existence of this uninhabited piece of sand. True, vacationers as a mass are herd animals and prefer to lie on the blanket next to other tan worshippers. But the human wave should seize every empty place following the law of connected vessels, in some unstoppable drive, which the successor of Sigmund Freud could describe as "lido libido". The very idea of a beach with no invisible lines connecting the pillars of windbreaks sounded absurd. It was like an empty window at the train station with a lone attendant, watching in reverie the hundreds of people queued up for other windows.

After we consumed the not quite edible dinner, we approached the reception desk of our center. The young girl was clearly terrified by our idea. She started to shout that we must not go to the empty beach, that no one comes back from there, that this is a bad place. Her face changed like in a kaleidoscope - grinning teeth flickered between appearing and disappearing smiles, strange expression lines wandered through the cheeks, causing us to shudder, her eyes closed and opened independently of each other. All we managed to find out was that that beach was inhabited by strange prehistoric creatures. And as it is common in dreams, the next scene took the four of us to a bottom of a rocky cliff. The strip of sand was not very wide, but it could easily accommodate dozens of sunbathing fans. We were alone here however, at least for a moment.

Suddenly the sea stopped humming, but the silence lasted only fractions of a second. We heard a terrifying rattling and we saw with astonishment that the waves continued through the sand and gravel.

Big reptiles jumped from among the sand waves. I recognized in them spinosaurs that I once wrote an article about. There is a theory that the reptiles belonging to this species, with the characteristic skin sail stretched out on the vertebral appendices, were the largest predators of the Cretaceous era. The finds from Morocco suggest that spinosaurs reached seventeen meters in length and a weight of over seven tons. But the giant lizards born of sand were not that big. They did not have to, because their number made up for it. Soon a dozen beasts surrounded us. We were convinced we were finished, when something very strange happened. The monsters heard something, because they turned their heads in one direction as if on cue. A yellow Cessna 150 was flying toward us from the direction of Łeba. The little plane was growing bigger, the growl was getting louder, and the dinosaurs began to stamp their feet in some prehistoric dance. To our astonishment, behind the controls of a flying machine we saw a gigantic rabbit in the aviator cap falling on his goggles... And then the real pandemonium began. The lizards tried to catch the brave aviator in their mouths, but he avoided them in a quadrille of acrobatics. Our joy was definitely premature though. It turned out that the reptiles can devour the elements of the reality that surrounds us, bite holes in the blue falling on us from the sky or sneaking to our feet with the crushing sea waves. One of the spinosaurs even tore off a piece of a nearby cliff with his teeth. At first, red lights shone in the holes left by the swallowed bites of the world, , but they soon dimmed down. A black mist began to float out of the holes in the reality, and I realized with horror that our world is just a thin patina on an immeasurable abyss. This abyss was pulling us in, while the spinosaurs continued their meal. And then everything faded, and even later, when we were falling into the blackness of the well, we realized that the wild beach was deserted and there were no dinosaurs or flying rabbits on it. And we were not there anymore either.

***

One of the worst nightmares happened to Martha a week after discovering the body in the attic. The worst thing about this dream was that it suggested awakening. Anyway, listen to what my wife wrote down that day:

"Wake up... Time to get up" - I hear my husband's voice floating in the air somewhere above my face. I do not have the strength to open my eyes, even though scraps of light are breaking through my eyelids. Marc speaks in a rather monotonous tone, which surprises me a little; he is usually perky and full of enthusiasm in the morning. However, I only mumble under my breath: "Five more minutes, give me a moment..." But he responds with a strange emphasis: "Honey, you must wake up immediately! Something terrible has happened!". I open my eyes and scream with fear. This is not Marc's face, but the face of a demon from the darkest corners of hell - red, peeling skin, bizarre protrusions on the cheeks, black eyes without irises or whites. This monster smiles at me... "Whaaat... what happened?" - I can hardly say a word. And Marc-NotMarc twists his lips, almost pushes his pin-sharp teeth out, and says: "Something terrible has happened! Your coffee is almost cold!" And then my husband leans over me and I close my eyes and I wake up for real...

I admit that I felt a bit uncomfortable after reading these words. Dreams began to invade our lives too much. Writing did not come easily to me that day - I remember that I was working on the latest law about taxes on supermarkets, and I had no idea how to elaborate my thesis. In a theory, it is about fair treatment of all market players, but the regulations will cause a collateral damage for all of us - as it always happens. Not to mention the fact that Polish retail chains will suffer the most from this change, because large foreign corporations are perfectly capable to handle any circumstances.

* * *

The dreams dazzled us with the richness of colors and boldness of visions, but how were we to interpret them? One day we decided to go to a soul doctor. Soon, however, it came to light that marriages that come together to the psychiatrist, automatically receive the label of "couples with problems". Then Martha came up with the idea of sending only me on the couch - after all, it was about dreams, not marriage therapy.

* * *

"It's a bizarre thought, but my life has lost its geography" - I smile at myself, and the distracted herds of neurons fall into panic, only to rush a moment later through the courtyard of the brain - the city on the very edge of the Indifference Plain. Their fear is absolutely unjustified - my smile is an inner smile and no face muscle will be involved. It is an unnecessary commentary on the overwhelming helplessness, a silent coda of the radio show of unfulfilled requests. Walking along the paths of a dream, I move between hanging curtains. "It is helplessness that is the darkest of nightmares in depression" - I think again, but this time I do not smile. And suddenly I regain consciousness. I am lying on a couch, not very comfortable, but looking like a comfortable one, oh how I would like Martha to be lying, stretched on a similar piece of furniture next to me. But I am here alone. The look-alike of the president, who certainly is not him, looks at me. A pure accident that the head of a psychiatric clinic looks like a well-known politician...

"You listen to the wrong melody," the doctor says, and I realize that I lost consciousness for just a few moments.

From behind his glasses, doctor Winicjusz Winnicki gives me a look that is familiar from the election posters of the ruling party.

"Do you know that I am friends with a well-known composer? - at least his voice is different from the indistinct baritone of the head of state. - He told me that the soundtrack subliminally determines the reception of the movie. Apparently, a psychological experiment was once made, in which the same film was accompanied by two completely different melodic lines. It was shown to two groups of viewers and it turned out that their opinions about the movie, and even the comprehension of its content, were also completely different..."

"What does this prove?" I interrupt him.

"The fact that you are still listening to the wrong melody. And it gives your life a definitely wrong direction."

To say that I am a bit lost is definitely an understatement. What the fuck is he talking about? On the other hand - maybe it's better that he does not talk about, for example, Danish sperm whales?

"Do you recommend enrolling in the conservatory for me, doctor? Or maybe downloading the correct soundtrack from the Internet?"

"Indeed, I have an idea how to help you. However, you must sign this document."

He gives me couple of sheets of paper decorated with the logo of the clinic.

"But what is this treatment supposed to be?" I still hesitate.

Winnicki now looks just like the father of the nation.

"It's an experimental therapy."

"I would like to know what I am actually getting myself in..."

The psychiatrist smiles under his mustache.

"Please, read the materials I gave you when you have time. You do not have to decide today. Will a week be enough?

A week of nightmares is definitely too long, but I can't make a decision without talking to Martha. We will read it in the evening.

***

Martha looked with me excitedly at the documents the psychiatrist gave me. With every minute, however, our faces got longer, the enthusiasm gave way to a growing shock. The text did not have any sense at all, it was a conglomeration of absurd sentences. I felt confused too. What could this shrink be doing?

"Oh my, I don't know. Maybe this writing follows the logic of dreams?" Martha asked uncertainly.

I only shook my head in disbelief.

"It's just gibberish. Although..." I stopped, clearly excited. "Look!"

I pointed triumphantly at the last paragraph of the printout. Martha read it aloud.

Thank you very much for reading this. The therapy has just begun. These sentences should trigger some mechanisms in the brain, which will shorten the treatment time significantly. I hope I have not discouraged you. According to the contract, we will meet at 7 pm on Thursday. Or maybe you would like to know something about the cause of your nightmares earlier? In that case, let's meet at the terminal of the tram 11 line on Monday at midnight. Regards, Vinicius Winnicki.

We thought it was a great joke. Martha said later that therapy could be interesting. However, I did not intend to roam around terminals and depots in the middle of the night. We both realized that we could easily wait until Thursday. However, it quickly turned out that the situation was changing dynamically.

***

In all this madness we had to make a considerable effort, which an attempt to spend time in a normal way proved to be. Board games with children, listening to the radio play list in the evening, dinner talks that distracted the dark fog that seemed to envelop our everyday life. Not to mention the work - it's not easy to do your job when you hear dead voices and feel someone dancing on your grave.

In the meantime, there have been terrorist attacks in Washington. It is as if the madness from Wietrzna Street spread to the whole world. We listened with growing disbelief to the press reports from the front line, which the capital of America has changed into. A few hundred victims, three suicide bombers, a perfectly synchronized action. It could not possibly happen, yet it was happening right before our eyes.

"It's not like it happened suddenly, you know?" Martha said at one point.

"What do you mean?"

"Oh, it's tempting to think that the world suddenly got crazy since we're going crazy too, you understand? But it has been going on for a long time, all the time, except the information doesn't reach us. We've just lived blissfully unaware till now..."

I shook my head.

"You talk as if our peaceful life was an illusion, an untrue being. But we live on various levels; this level of madness with which we have dealt recently is certainly not the norm..."

"But look, all these dead people. And this in Washington, no less. The whole world is immediately mourning, and meanwhile similar murders take place every day somewhere in Africa, in the Middle East. The arithmetic of sympathy, do you remember this poem?"

"Martha, darling, we can only try to live as before. That's all we can do, we can't give in to such sentiments."

"Except it's so difficult."

"I know."

I was supposed to write a text about raging commodity exchanges, so I soon went to my office. Martha also took to her own affairs. Everything else had to go to the back burner, get annihilated in the flow of oblivion. Then the evening reading by the beds of our little elves, night-time searching for new topics, and the night sleep that we were so afraid of. This way we held on to our refuge of normality, which slowly turned into the last, unconquered fortress.

Chapter 4

MARC AND MARTHA

Parents usually delude themselves that they are able to give their children the grace of a peaceful sleep. We also thought that we could save Sophie and Kallen from the ma͏ hat was tormenting us. We were wrong, as on many other accounts...

One evening, our crying son ran to our bed. We could not get out of him for a long time what kind of monster had visited him. It was only after several minutes that he began to tell us what he had dreamed of.

Kallen dreamed of a city, an empty city reminiscent of a model from the Cold War years, with frightening, though imperceptible figures walking the streets, where Silence and Muteness pop up suddenly instead of houses. He was running across this deserted scenery, pursued by a gigantic rubber duck. He did not know why an overgrown bathing toy was trying to catch him, but he could not let it do it. It could get him and change him into a rubber boy or something worse. At the same time, he had to watch out for invisible dinosaurs, whose heavy panting carried along the ravines of the streets. For some reason, these invisible monsters were not as terrifying as the giant duck; the loud breath of the great reptiles did not raise half of the horror of the quacking, multiplied by echo.

Kallen cried for a long time, cuddling up with me and Martha in turn. Finally, he fell asleep between us, his face gradually brightening up, as if our son wanted to calm down his concerned parents, show them that the nightmare is gone forever. And we were wondering about the whole story.

"Look, even the night fears can be innocent... Instead of decaying zombies, bloodthirsty cannibals or vampires, our son is afraid of rubber ducks," I tried to lighten things up.

"Eh... I mean... This is not a good topic for jokes. To tell you the truth, I'm panicking. Shit, these are our children, and we can't help them," Martha said.

Without a doubt, she was right. But something was bothering me. After all, we are usually afraid of what we do not know, the most frightening things are the faces of strangers, alien customs, the differences. Meanwhile, Kallen subconsciously gave the fear a familiar, or even friendly face. I came to the conclusion that it was even more terrifying. Perhaps in the next dream he will be running for his life away from us?

We decided together that I would go to a night meeting with Komorowski[*], I mean with Winnicki. We could no longer pretend we could deal with all this.

"Perhaps, just an idea, we should notify Sabol and Śmigielski?" My wife wondered.

"Yes, sure," I shuddered. "They probably already take us for mythomaniacs or even the mentally ill."

"You know, they both are also quite far from normal."

I smiled slightly.

"Normality is the statistical average of the social insanity."

Martha nodded.

"I am still a bit afraid of this therapist of yours..."

And I, as befits a man, did not confess to her that I had similar fears. Instead I hugged her tight, and then turned off the bedside lamp.

***

[*] Bronisław Komorowski, former president of Poland, whom Winicjusz Winnicki resembles

First of all, my wife, Martha. Firstly, my wife, secondly, the time of the day, which is wearing a foggy veil in spite of the full summer, but in the end it can be different in the morning.

Thus, firstly, my wife, secondly, the foggy veil, thirdly the water on the sheet, flowing with the current of all rivers through the oceans, all the rivers flowing under the sea surface, unrecognizable, and yet saying so much in so few words.

Firstly, my wife, secondly, the foggy veil, thirdly all the rivers of the world, fourth and fifth the fear, when we rush through empty streets, although we were prepared for this ride, all packed and in starting blocks, because it could happen at any time, but the fear is stronger because it is fourth and fifth, because she carries nine months of pregnancy in herself and infinitely long months of previous distress.

Thus, firstly my wife, secondly, the foggy veil, thirdly, the rivers of the world, fourthly, the fear, fifthly, the fear, sixthly, the room.

Firstly, my wife, secondly, the foggy veil, thirdly, the water on the sheet, fourthly, the fear, fifthly, the same, sixthly, the bright lit room, seventhly, the blood. The inevitable blood, rising with the breath of the surf waves on an invisible beach, blood as a harbinger of what is eighth and ninth, blood on which - like on a boat - you can sail to new waters, give them new names...

So, firstly my wife, secondly foggy veil, thirdly world rivers, fourthly fear, fifthly fear, sixthly, the lit room, seventhly, blood, eighthly, Kallen, ninthly, Sophie. It's you who gave meaning to the other digits, primers of long-forgotten alphabets, how wonderful that you came to us.

Ninthly and eighthly, you, seventhly, blood, sixthly, hospital room, fifthly and fourthly nonexistent anymore, thirdly world rivers, secondly misty veil, firstly my wife. Martha. You.

***

I am not very good at keeping my nerves in check, they usually get out of control, fortunately not in a detached, spasmodic, unintentional way. I was so damn scared for my husband, I did not know what this strange meeting would bring. And, of course, I fell asleep, and in my dream I came back to the land of nightmares. This time I ran as fast as I could through bleak wastes, chased by a bunch of mannequins. They moved like zombies, losing their limbs in a ghastly run, their wigs waving in the wind. I knew that there was no hiding place, that nothing would save me, neither help or helplessness. The mannequins were croaking with a strangely plastic cackle, like the voice of a cancer patient after a laryngectomy. They were getting closer, or maybe it was just the space that curved to my disadvantage in a mad act of destruction. The crazy puppets called me by name again and again, and I felt that this name was turning into a trap. Martha. Martha - has no luck, Martha - worthless, Martha - a torn-card. Martha - deceased*.

***

We are demons living in the walls of human homes. They call us in various ways - Black Harpists, Devourers of Dreams... This last term describes us quite accurately. What does our occupation look like? People often wake up in the morning and do not remember their dreams - they think they did not dream at all. But in fact it is completely different - we left the wall and ate their nightmares. We are beasts, we wear faces from the most terrible imaginations, but we do good... Because there are beings in the night-time lethargy that could drive everyone crazy. We do not allow this to happen. It is thanks to us that people do not even know what kind of fate they avoided.

SOMEONE ELSE IS DREAMING II

---

* Kid's teasing, these words rhyme with Martha.

51

How come such a strange nightmare, associated with zombies and Karol Dickens, came to me? I have no idea, I am just an ordinary IT specialist in a small family company...

Ah, how this New Year's night was dragging on! The last party-goers, caught up in the web of streets, returned home amidst broken bottles and lost confetti. Here and there, the remnants of firecrackers were burning up. The New Year had only ruled for three hours, and he already had a lot on his conscience.

The old man was running in the growing darkness. His face was distorted in a strange grimace, he gasped, but he knew he could not stop. He had realized it much earlier, when he was flying out of his empty apartment like a rifle bullet, trashing around in panic. There was very little time left. A correction - there was no time anymore. That is why he now trotted among the lengthening shadows, cut through the industrial landscape with the uneven rhythm of his feet hitting the pavement. The stalkers have not shown up yet, but the older man felt that it only gave a false sense of security. It is better to assume that they are just around the corner, that they follow him with young and sharp eyes.

Suddenly, his ear caught a suspicious sound coming from a nearby clump of trees. He glanced quickly toward it. Fortunately, it was just a dog-headed demon who devoured dead souls formed into the shapes of cats. Grandpa breathed a sigh of relief. For the time being he remained unthreatened.

***

You look at me as if I were the Oracle of the Seven Seas, the avatar of the Invisible House, or some fucking Kuba Wojewódzki*. You scream louder and louder.

"Why haven't they still caught him? Is it that hard to capture a dying old man?"

---

* TV personality

I do not rectify this information, after all you are well aware that - technically speaking - our man on the run has been dead for at least a few hours.

Besides, I understand your being pissed so well. After all, things used to be different. One took a new position with a clean account, no one demanded any compensation for past emotions. You could prove your own uniqueness, which resulted not only from the date on the stamps. And now? Everyone is demanding compensation for the lost opportunities, everyone drowns in sentimental memories. I sigh heavily, eh, where are our thick lines! And to think that the beloved Police only recently understood where the problem lies.*

"The problem is," I say "that there are more of them..."

Now you're really yelling at me like some possessed motherfucker.

"I'm sure they'll soon gather in a damn flock!"

I answer calmly that it is quite possible.

"Move your asses then, and slaughter them all!!!" You are yelling.

"Your wish is an order for me," I answer. "You're the New Year."

***

Indeed, the old man quickly found his soul mates, living outside the mainstream of the city. A dozen grandpas already were warming their butts up by the bonfire made in the partial shadow of an old bridge. Every now and then one of them jumped up, joining the procession wandering around the flickering flames, and then his distorted face contorted ominously. Each of the characters was affected by some visible disability, the skin was disfigured by open wounds, sometimes rotting. At one point, one of the most time-bitten gentlemen began to dance, holding the growing garlands of intestines in his hands. The guts fell on the dirty earth like broken balloons, but the old man seemed completely unaware of the situation. He was still

---

* see https://en.wikipedia.org/wiki/Thick_line

making awkward steps imitating a dance, but being a parody of this dance. The youngest of the old men, who only a few minutes ago was just a wild game, now mumbled something cheerfully under his breath. Others, further ahead in their decomposition, were unable to produce understandable messages. In an inharmonious chorus, only one word repeated with an alarmingly high frequency...

"Bbbbbrrrrains..."

* * *

"So they turn into zombies." You narrow your eyes, staring at your helpers. "I will probably also end up like them one day."

No one dares to deny or confirm this bold hypothesis. In fact, it is not known how zombies are created, what brings them to life (notice what a convoluted construction I used in this phrase!). In the past, they did not multiply as much, but it was before the world rotated one time too many, as my father says, or before the world went forward, as uncle Stefan says.

Well, such an undead year can make a lot of mess. In the old days, years simply passed, melting slowly in the memory, we remembered them later, reviewing photos or overdue bills. Safely or not, we closed the galleries of completed or abandoned expeditions, we burned our bridges or rocked on their high spans.

However, for some time now, the years have been coming back to life, and it brought about a lot of perturbations. Above all, with memory. Memories, which should be more or less painlessly obliterated, suddenly came back with blind stubbornness. In addition, they were intense and intrusive, which was not associated with any beneficial effect. Because - let's agree - there are less happy years that we would all rather forget.

And from the New Year's point of view it was much worse. The guy had some plans, he tried to carry out his ideas, and here it turned out that everything returns to the state from a dozen months before.

In addition, everyone has the right to a clean slate. Later, things can go in various directions - we cover it with checkered intellectual notes or festoons of insignificant scribbles - but the beginning and the first opportunity are available to everyone. Meanwhile here - surprise! - such injustice...

I am not surprised therefore that you are angry at the sluggishness of the Police and the secret agents. I am even less shocked by your joy, when in a dozen or so seconds you will hear that the hounds have tracked the escapee.

***

At first, the Old Year did not hear the sounds of the chase. His predecessors had even less chance for that, as their hearing aids were often completely destroyed. The entry of an armed phalanx equipped with fighting clubs and stun guns soon decimated the ranks of the living dead.

The Old Year had to flee alone again. And although, despite everything, he was convinced that he owed his existence to some bizarre aberration of nature, he could not accept the inevitability of his fate. After all, people who are in a vegetative coma, also become a medical phenomenon when they wake up after a few weeks or even years. How to ultimately distinguish their fate from what happened to him? At the basic level of perception, he assumed that he became just a miraculously revived dead man. But there was also the other side of the coin - precisely these patients who woke up from the coma. How was he different from them? Well, maybe he smelled a bit more intensely, but he could certainly find couple of patients who exude more stinking miasma. If, therefore, we accept the practical indistinguishability of both fragrant types, then murdering zombies was no different from euthanasia. From here, it is not far to the very heart of the matter - at least that's what the Old Year contemplated, while running for his life from the place of execution. New Year's soldiers systematically eliminated the resistance of the trembling dead people - because it is only in fairy tales for children and horrors that zombies appear dangerous. The dead are defenseless when facing the living - it is worth remembering this aphorism.

The Old Year was running and did not hear the chase approach yet. He twisted and turned in the alleys shrouded in shadows, hid under the eaves, over which the merciful mist hung its veils. Well, it was only a borrowed time, but before he would leave forever, he wanted to leave something to remember him by, so as not to be ashamed before the past generations.

But this wandering was not an aimless and panicked retreat, just to get as fast and far as possible in order not to hear the hunters' shouts. The Old Year was heading towards the headquarters of his successor.

***

You are slowly getting reports from all search groups. The laboratories deliver samples of the plasma that leaked from the exterminated rebels. But you are focused all the time on the only goal that has so far escaped all pursuits. You think about the cursed forerunner. A distorted face, which you will never show in your photos and holoportraits, looks at me crookedly.

"You probably see me as a paranoiac. You smile ironically.".

"You know well that it is not my business to judge," I think loudly. "But it's not paranoia, rather some form of the Oedipus complex..."

"For heavy eons! Don't treat this guy as if he were my father!" Apparently I have hit a nerve. "He is at most your former boss who occupied my position at work previously. Let's call him a harbinger, but not a father, damn it!"

I am looking at this youngster who will never have a childhood, who carries all his traumas gathered at the bottom of his eyes. How much he felt hurt by this situation in which he must kill his own, umm, progenitor?

"Let's call him any way you like, New Year. You know very well that there is no one truth, there are only different methods of perceiving it," I explain.

You bring the asymmetrical smile on your young-old face again. "You did not have enough time to practice your facial expressions" - I think to myself. Anyway, the New Year does not see his reflection in the mirror.

"He's coming here, isn't he?" The corners of your lips tremble, as if they couldn't decide what shape to form. In this light, your smile begins to resemble closing gates.

"And you will be waiting for him here," I answer. "Doesn't it always happen in the same way?"

* * *

He was giving off a barely perceptible smell of decomposition around himself. "Zombie? I am some kind of an ephemerid, not a zombie!" - he thought bitterly as he stood before the entrance to the mirrored skyscraper. The wind, faithful to morbid customs, moaned and wandered around and around the buildings, and looked with its invisible fingers for a gap through which it could squeeze inside. Its efforts were futile - modern office buildings are resistant to this type of tests. However, the interior of the skyscraper was empty, everybody seemed to have disappeared. It was puzzling, considering the paranoid character of the New Year. The old man was ready for a confrontation with armed guards, without thinking about his chances in such a situation. Perhaps he would be able to dodge the rounds of the bullets in a matrix-like style, or maybe he would just kill them all with laughter? Fortunately, he did not have to worry about it anymore. And yet the desolated lobby was very suspicious. "The son of the gun probably knows that I'm on my way to get him" - it crossed his mind. Let things go this way then. They were thick as thieves, both of them could recite the opponent's weaknesses and strengths when awakened in the middle of the night. But the older one had the advantage of experience, and was aware of something that his heir had no right to know. The trick is not in learning the weaknesses of the enemy, guessing what he is most afraid of. The real talent is to recognize what gives the enemy the greatest pleasure. Only then can you subject him to the most devious torture.

***

If your age were measured on a simple human scale, you would be over eighteen years old. Later, when time will go on, you will grow older at the rate of four mortal years for each month of the reign. So you are in excellent physical condition and you do not have to be afraid of your predecessor in this respect. You jump onto the conference table and wave the Nordic walking poles. The room is slowly filled with the smell bringing to mind the old rotting leaves and the meat gone bad.

Even though your predecessor died just a few hours ago, he seems to be a very far gone corpse, exhumed and resurrected by a madman. This animated carcass stands to face the bronze muscles and the violent rage of the competitor. And it will turn out any moment, on whose side the Zeitgeist is playing today.

So you stand facing each other like poor imitations of gunmen from the Wild West.

"You came to me?" You throw a contemptuous glances at the competitor, weary of life. "But your time has just passed!"

"I was a man in my prime!" You can almost hear the echoes of knight's songs and flapping of banners in the old man's cries. And then Old Year, shuffling his feet, approaches his successor.

You circle the lobby for a few moments, waiting for some mysterious sign. Then there is quite an unexpected turn of events, and ghosts and specters enter the stage...

***

You imagine it's such a cool job, don't you? So, first of all, you know shit, if you think so, that's what! I will not even mention the entire New Year's progeria, the galloping petrification of the brain, this accelerated aging, which at the position of the months' conductor must be taken with all the benefits of an inventory. But let's also take into account these slightly better hidden motifs, which grow under the pretense of order, like invisible vermin. Let's take the immortal wishes, that you repeat completely thoughtlessly. Remember? While the statement "may this year be happy for you and auspicious for those who depend on you" sounds potentially dangerous, others are much more dangerous. For example this, "may each following year be happier than the previous..." It always comes effing true, get it? So for the Year currently in office, such wishes are as pleasant as the ancient curse.

Surprisingly, we hear the toll of bells hanging somewhere in the invisible tower made of air. A rhythmic and deep pulsation, carried over our heads, which themselves turn into concert carillons because of the vibrations. And then only the dull pain exploding behind the eyes, displaying bloody afterimages on the pupils' screens. These penetrating strikes cease without warning and a shining rain falls on us. These are not drops, they are little winged figures with ugly faces, fallen angels of the microcosm. After a while, I realize that my first judgment was too harsh - because it is a statistical normality rather than ugliness, but because of that, it is unrealistic. After all, elves and flying ghosts should dazzle us with their beauty, enchant with unearthly, aesthetic proportions. Do not believe that beauty is in the eyes of the beholder - I have seen many eyes that had literally nothing enchanting in them.

Fairies with the faces of commoners start to circle around both competitors. The bells toll again in the depths of our skulls. Old and New Years sneak around each other, always keeping a safe distance. And then I hear a cold voice that seems to be coming from inside of my skull, although the boy and the old man are also aware of it. The bell says:

"When the Old Year dies and the New one comes, the ghost bells start to toll. Whoever heard them, will never stop thinking about them, they will come back to him, emerging from behind the colonnade of other sounds, popping up unexpectedly in the middle of an operatic aria or a guitar solo. But as long as these bells, which called us to come again, keep tolling, as long as we are spinning here in a dance, different versions of the future are justifiable. However, when the last gong resounds in the thinning air, only one of you will remain in the circle. Fight then!"

They went at each other. Blood spurts as Old's jaw clenches on New's neck in melee, and at the same time, the knife of his opponent pierces the stomach of the living corpse. The drops of red falling to the ground flicker like beads, and the amused ghosts circle around them, jumping wildly. There is more and more blood, it squirts with waterfalls from the bitten arteries and dissected aortas. The fight does not last long. Soon two senseless bodies are lying on the dance floor. Uh oh!

Before the implications of this fact fully reach me, the voice speaks again.

"Only you are left... There is no other way, you take over the responsibilities of the minister of days..."

The melody of the chimes stops and the silence ensues. The dancing ghosts disappear somewhere, the bodies of the dead turn into ashes. I'm left alone. Have you guessed that all the elements of my plan have just been fulfilled? The hardest thing was to summon the zombies, and the rest - easy-peasy! A bit of a subtle manipulation, a proper reconnaissance of the opponent, a stroke of luck.

You think that I have to be a dumb loser if I have decided to accept such an ungrateful function, because I condemned myself to less than twelve months of life, after which the inevitable end of the clouds will come. Well, many things can change during a year. I've really thought of everything to the smallest details. I will tell you one thing - you will not recognize this place in three hundred and sixty-five days. I can promise you that. Happy New Year!

Chapter 5

MARC AND MARTHA

I went to the tram terminal, in a tram, of course. The last tram. I would love to write that something disturbing happened to me on the way, that some freaks watched me ove wspapers they were reading, or some young muscle men roughed me up. Nothing like this happened, I was alone with the driver on the tram, which looked completely normal. In spite of this, I felt a lot of discomfort and anxiety. Perhaps because, in spite of the late hours, it was so... normal. Sometimes it is normality and mundanity that bring out the darkest thoughts. I got off the streetcar straight into the empty street, as if I moved to Kallen's dreams due to some mysterious magic.

I was once at my friend's writer's evening. I remember that I asked what scares him the most. He replied after a moment's thought, that a blank sheet was the most scary - it is not about a writer's block though, but on the contrary - about the vastness of possibilities. The most terrible monster is the one that is still toothless, the light that begins to dim, the dying buzz, wrapping itself in a shroud of silence.

So I got off the streetcar. I looked around, but my psychiatrist was nowhere to be seen. I set off towards a distant bus stop shelter, carefully avoiding puddles; the candles of the street lamps were burning out somewhere in the distance, and the singing of Leonard Cohen dispersed the silence. There was a woman in an evening gown sitting under the shelter I was approaching, To my astonishment, I recognized in a stranger Vinicius Winnicki.

"Don't be surprised... I can't afford being recognized," he began to explain. The blond wig on his head contrasted strangely with the mustache and glasses. And his dress? It was only from up close that it lost its elegance, transforming into an outfit of a woman of not strongly guarded virtue. I began to wonder what this all was about.

"You must be wondering what this all is about," Winnicki interrupted my thoughts brutally. "This disguise is an element of therapy... Mine, not yours... Please do not pay attention to it."

I responded with a forced smile and a nod. I was not able to say a single word.

"You came here to understand where the dreamy horrors that plague your family are coming from, right?"

I nodded in silence again.

"You probably never heard of the Black Harpists?" He smirked at me.

"Is this some death metal band?" I was finally able to speak.

"Poor shot. A bad miss," said the doctor. "Black Harpists are the protagonists of many folk tales and legends. The Bible also mentions them, though in a veiled way. According to the legend, they live in the walls of houses inhabited by people, and feed on their dreams. They usually devour our nightmares, so that we do not go mad. The researchers from Neider's group in Leiden tried to solve their mystery, as well as numerous crooks from American universities. They have never become the object of interest of serious scientists however."

"I think I know why," I replied. "I have never heard such nonsense in my life."

"A man of little faith," Winnicki's smile was simply captivating. I wondered if it had anything to do with his costume. "Can't you see that everything fits together? The guardian of your dreams has been murdered and scary horrors have been terrifying you ever since."

"So he was a Black Harpist? He looked more like an ape-man," I cut him off mockingly.

"According to the knowledge that has been accumulated about these beings, they are somewhat removed from the general canons of beauty. Neider claims that they come from a different dimension, and above all, they are relics of old times. Are you aware for how long the humanity has known the phenomenon of a dream?"

"I am sure you will tell me..."

"As you can guess, dream books appeared already in ancient Egypt and Babylon, in an attempt to interpret the symbolism of dreams. One can notice that practically every culture has believing in the meaning of dream visions in its tradition. In the Gospel, it is in a dream that Joseph sees an angel who reveals the birth of the Son of God to him. There have been prophet dreams, which influenced the history. Oneiromancy, or the divination based on dreams, was the domain of not only soothsayers, but also great philosophers. Hippocrates wrote a work in which he connected dreams with diseases. Such thinkers as Aristotle or Cicero were also familiar with this field."

"So we have been dreaming since forever," I was already slightly impatient with this lecture. "But where are the Black Harpists in this whole story?"

-"Said Hippocrates believed that there exist both healing dreams and those that lead to illness. He thought that unknowable beings watch over us, protecting us from the sinister influence of the latter."

"Fantastic!" I've had enough of this tirade. " Our guardian angels are the Neanderthals living among the clay cinderblocks, is that right?"

Winnicki was playing with a strand of his artificial hair.

"Perhaps it sounds like a madman's dream, but I assure you that the reality is full of much more queer things."

"Okay. Let's make the absurd assumption for a moment that I believe your words. Who, in your opinion, killed this Black Harpist?"

"The Purple Drummer," he looked at me for a moment, and his smile was getting wider. "I'm kidding! I fooled you, wow! I have no idea who murdered the resident of your house, but I know something else."

"Namely?"

"Namely, if you do not find it out quickly, your whole family will end up in a psychiatric hospital, or something even worse will happen to you."

I hesitated. The situation had all the features of absurdity, but there was a brightness on Winnicki's face that made me believe in what he had been telling. Well, I just hoped it was not a highlighting powder. Although I should have already known that a makeup is sometimes a deadly camouflage that lures its victims into a trap.

* * *

I did not believe a single one of his words. My husband, apart from his many virtues, has been endowed with a whole arsenal of defects, with credulity in the first row among them. I was beginning to seriously worry about the whole situation. As Bard Mlynarski sang: "I have known your reasons from reports for some time. They are so sharp oh oh... Friend, what do you need them for? Look at the situation we are in... at the moment!"" At the same time, I felt some dissonance that yanked my soul, some inadequacy of the situation.

How could I believe in the demons living in the walls and feeding on the crumbs of our dreams?

I heard that a large percentage of psychiatrists are eligible for treatment in isolation wards - apparently Winnicki was in accordance with this street's wisdom. Why could not Marc assess this impartially? I came to the conclusion that my husband wanted so desperately to find a solution to the problem tormenting us, that

---

* A song "Situation" by Wojciech Młynarski

he was willing to accept far-reaching compromises with his own common sense.

"If you want, I'll look for information on these creatures from the wall at the library," I said conciliatorily.

"You probably think it's all the foulest rubbish..."

"It may be worth checking, though," I replied. And after some thinking, I realized that I indeed thought so. I hugged him, astonished once again that it is so warm and safe in Marc's arms.

"I will show you tonight how to hide the sky in hands," my husband murmured.

And I believed him again.

***

She did not believe me, I could feel it in my guts, there was disbelief in her embrace, in every caress and kiss. But I was also doubtful because I did not accept the words of my psychiatrist-transvestite uncritically. What is faith and trust anyway? It's accepting that we do not have to examine anything anymore, it's a loss of interest in a given subject. If you trust me, it does not mean that you accept everything that I have to say without reservation. If you believe in something, then you do not stop trying to see it with your own eyes. Perhaps now I have made a mental misuse by combining a strictly religious term with the mundane side of life. But prose does not exclude poetry, it complements it - and it is a two-way relationship. And somewhere in this equation, between the prose of everyday life and the poetry of an embrace in the evening, love wanders, which causes that this equation has no solution, that its function can't be drawn in any coordinate system.

Was Winnicki a madman? Or maybe we also started a free fall in a well of madness? On the other hand, I did not want to get too deep into the psychiatrist's actions. In the end, he himself admitted that his outfit was part of the therapy, and besides, I did not want to make him a leading character in my life.

***

The observer wonders about the further development of the events, his thoughts waver around possible scenarios, according to which the investigation will go. An unusual investigation, because he is well aware who murdered his friend. It was the Whites' doing, but why did they brake the Treaty after all these centuries of the truce? Years used to last a long time in their bronze immobility once, now they turned into fleeting moments, which can't be made sense of. "The world has moved forward," the observer thought, not realizing that he was quoting a well-known writer of horrors. He must quickly explain the ambiguity, listening to delicate sounds of the harps, polyphonic and polysemic. Except that he has not the slightest idea how to do it... He may have to rely on the ingenuity of the inhabitants of the abandoned house.

Chapter 6

SABOL

ommissioner Sabol speaking "I said, but only an automatic voice replied to me, offering credit, policy, holiday or other bulshit. You cannot run away from son   technological achievements, they are inevitable. Just like being in this stifling room on the floor occupied by the investigation squad."

There is no boy who would not want to be a policeman at a certain age. I've always wanted to be an actor. Life went on a different course, but I usually don't complain. In this I clearly differ, fuck, I can even say, distinctively differ, from the colleagues who lament on the work schedule, dilapidated police cars, overdue inflation raises, the superiors, the subordinates and, most of all, on today's youth with their ACAB message. I listen stoically to these complaints about earnings, blood, sweat and tears in the private grange of the district commander. I know how to wash this whole shell off myself - when I take off my uniform in the evening, I change into a normal person. Anyway - what is normality, if not the statistical average of social insanity, as someone once remarked - I can never remember names, which sometimes gets me in trouble.

However, I am primarily an actor - so you can't believe everything that you hear from me. Sometimes I think that acting resembles telling stories, or showing magic tricks. The audience is perfectly aware that they are taking part in a play that is, by definition, detached from reality. Everyone knows that this woman has not really been cut in half, that the flashes from the mirrors are not sparks of magic, that you are not a fucking Hamlet, but an actor who has just graduated. And yet, every viewer wants to believe that magic really exists, that the girl will return to her undivided form only through witchcraft, that he is looking at the real Danish prince. And where is the job in the Police in all that? Simple, you need to make money somehow, not too impressive anyway.

Someone knocked on my room door.

"Open, no?" I shouted at the door. It was Śmigielski. "What's up? I asked in a concise style.

"You would never guess... Do you remember that disappearing dead man in the Majewski's house? We got a report about him."

"Tell me that's a joke, no?"

"Maybe, but we should investigate the matter. Somehow I don't think this couple would talk right and left about the dead troglodyte, who dissolved in the air. And yet the matter has apparently leaked outside."

I shrugged.

"Show me this report. It's probably anonymous."

Śmigielski's eyes widened.

"Yes and no. The letter was signed by a WW"

I laughed.

„Maybe Wojciech Waglewski*, no?"

"I don't think so, anyway, read it."

I noticed with astonishment that the note was handwritten. It would be a great sample for the police graphologist, but the last expert was fired six months ago. Cutting costs - you know. The management of the company found, quite rightly, that the demand for similar expertise decreased drastically in the era of printouts and e-mails. Interestingly, almost exactly the same argument was made for the reduction of jobs in a unit dealing with computer crime. However, since they stopped investing in computers, police hackers became to be needed. Well, never mind, I was supposed not to complain about anything. I looked at the words written:

---

* Polish musician, WW is pronounced like the name of his band, Voo Voo.

I know what happened to the deceased from the Majewski apartment. He ended up in the Skeletons Lake... It's not a joke. I would gladly share my knowledge about this subject with the Police. I remain at your disposal, W.W.

Śmigielski was smiling under his breath.

"It's some madman, why didn't you throw it in the trash?" I asked, irritated.

"I've tracked down our mysterious informer. It was quite difficult, but..." he was clearly pleased with himself.

"Never mind the details, no?" I interrupted. "Who wrote it?"

"A certain Winicjusz Winnicki, I know him well," Śmigielski replied. "He's a psychiatrist whom I stopped for illegal practice after he lost his professional license. Quite a figure. You know, he never admitted his mistake, claiming he had been the victim of unjustified and unfair accusations."

"Do you know why they took his license away?" I was curious.

"It's also a good story. Imagine that a few years ago, our Vice stopped him. It turned out that the doctor was dressing up as a woman, and then he picked up guys in bars. The matter got public, a psychiatric areopagus gathered, and then his license was revoked. In my humble opinion, it was not even about Winnicki's unusual sexual habits, but the attempt to sweep it under the carpet. The guy simply lost his marbles. This is supposedly frequent for doctors of this specialty."

"And now suddenly our transvestite psychiatrist somehow gets access to the details of the secret investigation we've been carrying out, right?"

"You're right, it's a strange thing."

I looked thoughtfully at my friend.

"We have to interrogate him. But how to determine his whereabouts?"

Śmigielski shrugged.

"Perhaps we can use the business card attached to the letter?"

I burst out laughing. Indeed, tracking down our informer required a really devilish mastering of the art of deduction from Śmigielski.

***

Clothed in armor, I rode on a quick-legged steed, and my name aroused terror. The sword that hung at my side was not a dummy weapon - many enemies had already learned it; their souls howled, chained to the walls of the Forgotten City. A wonderful feeling - to be a hero in the land of commoners. I was solving the mystery of a murder committed in a medieval abbey. The victim was a young girl, with the blood of the Venetian gondoliers flowing in her veins. This case was a real challenge - a chamber with a body locked from the inside, a mirror dagger stuck in the heart, throwing bloody reflections on the wall. Before that I landed on a distant planet, I was researching the composition of the atmosphere, I was discovering the secrets of an extinct civilization... I was a passive detainee of fictitious worlds, a multitude of forms, an endless gallery of colorful portraits.

Bulshit, I was none of that. I did not manage to become an actor. I was just myself. But I do not like to complain, I do not complain about my fate. There is no boy who would not want to be a policeman at a certain age.

***

We invited our former psychiatrist to come at 3pm. Strangely - he arrived punctually. Even stranger - he was dressed in a classic suit, ironed pants and a double-breasted jacket and a string tie, one of those that were fashionable twenty years ago in country ceremonies. But what struck me most was Winnicki's similarity to a very famous figure from the heights of power. This impression faded immediately however, as soon as the interrogated doctor began to answer our questions.

"Where is it, no, this Lake of Skeletons?" I had to ask about it at the very beginning.

Winnicki was sitting hunched in a chair. He looked at me with amused eyes.

"Why, are you planning to go there? This place is inaccessible to mortals and is located in the wall of the Majewski's house..."

"What do you mean in the wall?" Śmigielski interrupted. "Are you spinning some fairy tales?"

-"Funny that you used this expression, Commissioner," the psychiatrist laughed. "You must be really interested in folk tales..."

"Enough of that! " This time I had it with him. "We'll go there after the interrogation, no? And now tell us, how do you know about the alleged murder on Wietrzna Street?"

That damn lunatic, motherfucker, and rogue in one only twisted his face in another half-smile.

"Ask the Majewski..."

Darn, I felt that he knew much more than he was revealing to us. If only I did become an actor, I would now be riding a horse in a film studio against a blue-screen and I wouldn't give a rat's ass about all the investigations of this world! And he begins to tell a bizarre story about the guys living in the walls, about the harps they play - these sounds take them to our reality, so that they can watch over the peaceful sleep of its inhabitants, fuck, what a bunch of crap! In my opinion, this guy qualifies for an immediate move to a psych ward.

Śmigielski records everything diligently as if he did not trust the voice recorder on the desk. He is right, I once got fooled by this soulless device myself. Since then, I use, as the computer scientist would say, "an analog backup" of a digital recording. Fuck, what a stranger I am to this place! My destiny was the theater stage, adoration of the audience, maybe a television career? Meanwhile, I have to listen to the crap of an old fart dressed in a classically elegant suit... If I wanted to, I could turn on the TV and listen to the double of our interrogated delinquent making an equally untrue statement to the nation.

"That would be all, thank you," I finally put a stop to this absurd verbal diarrhea. I wanted to add the formula about not leaving the city, but I bit my tongue. When he left, I looked at my subordinate.

"So what do you think about all this?" I asked.

"He's quite a storyteller," Śmigielski answered. "But I gonna make some research through my secret channels, maybe I will find something about these Dark Harpists, or whatever their name is... This name reminds me of a gang, maybe we are dealing with trading of hallucinogenic drugs here?"

"That would certainly explain a lot. They killed the dealer, they quickly removed the body... We have to visit the Majewski again, perhaps this case is not as stupid as it seemed to us, no?"

"When will we go to them?"

For a moment, I thoughtfully bit the ends of my non-existent mustaches. It was not easy at all, but as a would-be actor, I was able to deal with such a challenge.

"Tonight will be best," I was thinking loudly. "If we are dealing with a group of drug dealers, we can't waste time, no? We almost ran out of it anyway."

And that's what we did.

***

The observer sits at the shore of the Skeleton Lake. The sun always sets in this land, it immerses its red tuchus in the darkening waters for twenty-four hours a day. From time to time, the campfires of the travelers - stuck between the dark and the dawn, yet constantly staring at the endless sunset - lit up on the waterside. Sometimes the water carries the voices of the Singers, occasionally accompanied by Harpists. But today the observer is alone here. He stares at the water, marked with red sparks, and then closes his eyes, open for too long. Then the lake disappears.

SOMEONE ELSE IS DREAMING III

I worked as a veterinarian... It kind of explains my first dream tonight.

My dear friend, do not throw this letter too hastily. I would like to explain to you why you must have an Armadillo Breeder's Set. These are just a dozen sentences that, believe me, will change your life beyond recognition. Even though there is a shortage of things of which we could say they are necessary in today's world. Many so-called salesmen knock on your door, trying to sell you pretty and impractical things. Others present with incomprehensible pride the products that could be useful if they did not offend our aesthetic sense. What to do? Throw them out the door!

The Japanese company Phil-Lips (not to be confused with Phillips) is introducing a new, sensational product to the Polish market. It is the Armadillo Breeder's Set! It is an absolutely complete application, which is characterized by a high degree of compatibility with other similar products. However, it is more ideal than them! What's more, it is a new link in computer evolution!

At this moment, there is probably a slight doubt in your mind - why do I need such a set, if I am not an armadillo breeder, actually I do not even breed any animals? This is a completely wrong reasoning. Each of us is a armadillo breeder in exactly the same way, in which a computer owner becomes partly an IT specialist! You can't turn away from the mirror, my dear friend, in the vain belief that the world behind you will disappear.

Ease of use of our product means that everyone becomes immediately an expert in the matters of growing and breeding armadillos. The user-friendly interface is the particularly valued advantage of the product, but the possibility to extend the whole configuration later may also be the selling point. The problem of dosing the daily portion of feed is solved in a very interesting way, with the use of virtual reality technology. Another novelty is the cloning option, which will allow you in the future to create exact duplicates of our armored pets.

Other companies involved in the production of similar, although defective, gadgets often accuse us of a serious marketing mistake. "Where can people get these armadillos?" They ask sneeringly. - "This are rare animals, doomed for a fast extinction, that do not live in Poland at all," I would like to strongly deny such rumors here. Armadillos are like Fiat Multipla - there are so many of them that we no longer pay attention to them. We suggest a small experiment. Please look around your workplace - you will surely see at least one armadillo.

Armadillos, or Dasypodidae, are great domestic animals, irreplaceable play companions of small children and faithful friends of the adults. These are quiet and exceptionally clean creatures, and in addition, able to remove unwanted inhabitants from our homes, such as ants and termites. The product we offer gives you the chance to shape the psyche of the little armadillos. Well-designed packages of application software offer an option of choosing the type of training (defense armadillo, hound armadillo, armadillo - guide of the blind). Of course, you do not have to use them at all. The armadillo may remain a domestic pet who will pay off with the eternal gratitude of his armored heart for casual care and a little tenderness.

"Why not a dog or a cat?" - you will probably ask. Just look at the cost calculation (delivered upon payment of the initial fee). Armadillos are much cheaper to use, and at the same time much more pleasant to touch. Japanese scientists have shown that stroking the calcium-saturated horny-bone armor greatly relieves stress. More conservatively minded owners can pat the animal's hairy belly.

If you have already made a decision, submit your order to the address below. The first two hundred entries (the order is determined by the date of the postmark confirmed by an owl's pellet) will be rewarded with an enriched Armadillo Breeder Set! It will include a special termitiere shaped feeder and a virtual leash. Wishing you lots of fun using our set...

***

Deeply disturbed by the plague of the flock of homeless armadillos roaming around our villages and towns, we would like to express our deepest indignation with the emergence of the so-called Armadillo Breeder Set, disseminated by Phil-Lips.

It is a well-known fact that armadillos are disgusting creatures, completely alien to our cultural setting. This is a thoughtless copy of a stupid American trend for a closer-to-nature life. In vain shall we seek these animals on the pages of Henryk Sienkiewicz's books or in the ballads of our national bard - Mickiewicz Adam. They are even absent in Jan Kochanowski's works. It is just another American invention, after the so-called Halloween and Valentine's Day. A group of crooks, perhaps taking advantage of Polish deeply rooted fondness for the TV series about the four tank men*, is in fact trying to cut us off from our national roots.

The creatures unknown to the Polish tradition are to deprive the guide dogs of their jobs, and replace the joyful barking with mindless whining at hunting events, so widespread today. A soulless and secular technique, hidden under a hard armor, enters in place of a feeling and faithfulness. The company Phil-Lips certainly impresses with its mastering of the newspeak and pseudo-scientific jargon. Let us not be flooded with a stream of meaningless words. Let's protect

---

* "The four tank men and a dog" TV series; tank men and armadillo are words with the same roots (pancerz-armour) in Polish (pancerni-tank men, pancernik-armadillo) *our language, so that we would not see etymological monstrosities appear in a few years, like "call the armadillos off" or "in the armadillohouse"! And what would the title "Four tank-men and armadillo" look like?*

In the leaflet circulated by Phil-Lips, we found a following statement: "Each of us is an armadillo breeder (...)". We want to deny it with absolute certainty - we are not! The real Poles can't be them! We live in a free country where everyone can breed what he likes. Of course, within reason. What if, say, everyone wanted to keep a camel? Because it was the previous system, that enslaved us with generalizations and treating everyone according to a single pattern. Let's not allow the return of similar practices, slipping in under the guise of Japanese or American democracy.

We can share the results of the research, which clearly shows that armadillos carry many infectious diseases. Some of them are incurable! For the sake of your children's health, isolate the potential carriers until the arrival of the special group, appointed by us. In such difficult times, we have to stay together.

We announce a boycott of all Phil-Lips and Phillips products (just in case!). We order the destruction of all copies of the Armadillo Breeder Set, computers and laptops, and even mobile phones. Let's be merciless.

***

Sometimes the death of a pet moves us more than the departure of a human being - as if we witnessed a death of an angel. My beloved armadillo gave up the spirit after almost twenty years of living together. Always tender and sensitive, he knew how to infect me with his optimistic approach to life. To this day I can hear his purring, when I gently pushed the cold air to his ears, forming a fan with my fingers. I remember with affection how happily he retrieved my prosthetic hand I threw for him. It was not easy to part after such a long time. I cried all night long, and the morning came gray and hard like an armor. Well, what can we do, that's vis maior... I always wanted to try an armadillo soup.

And then I woke up in the middle of the night... My next dream was much stranger.

I dreamed that I found myself in a small town near Warsaw, where the forests were intertwined with the streets, the dogs barked behind fences once louder, once more quietly, and the pedestrians did not resemble those rats on boosters from the city. Interestingly, I had absolutely no idea where my knowledge about the geographical location of this place came from. In any case, I came to this place by accident - maybe I did not get off at the right stop, or maybe I just missed it, staring at the object in my lap? It often happens to me - I am sitting on the bus reading a book and I do not notice my stop. They say it is a real compliment for a writer who could create a world so complete, that the stimuli from reality no longer reach the reader.

I got out and noticed a map. It marked out long lines of unknown streets and foreign names, revealing the mysterious contours of the parts of the town I had never heard of before. I looked around the empty alley. I had no idea where I was... To say that I was in a panic, would be an understatement. Maybe I ended up in a strange ghetto, unknown to the cartographers from my world? How was I supposed to get out from here? I started walking down the street, and after a few minutes I got to the intersection with a statue in its center, depicting an old soldier sitting together with two girls on a bench. Where did I end up and how can I get out of this dream? The simplest method, that is awakening, somehow did not occur to me. I smiled to myself, and the distracted herds of neurons panicked, to run along the brain courtyards a moment later. Absolutely nothing justified their fear - my smile was an internal smile, and no face muscle was involved in it.

Walking along the paths of the dream, I moved between the fleeing cyclists and runners, but decided not to pay any attention to them. At one point I stopped to think about how to proceed. I was standing next to a massive, green building, there was quite a thick forest on the other side of the road. Something flashed between the neurons once again. How did I know this house?

Then I heard voices from behind the fence. Curious, I looked into the garden and saw a handsome guy with two children - they had to be about ten years old and had inexhaustible sources of youthful energy in their breasts. I stared at the three of them, understanding more and more that I also lived in this house, that these were my children and my husband, that everything that I took for a real life before my getting to sleep, was not at all a reality, but a bizarre prison. For my lonely life in a loft as a declared single is a delusion, my work for one of the major consulting companies - an untruth, everything that I remember from the times before I fell asleep - an illusion.

And now I had only one wish - to enter this hospitable house, to take the girl and the boy, and then you, into my arms. To not wake up anymore.

Chapter 7

VINICIUS

It does not help me at all to be a look-alike of the former president... A few days ago I saw a patient suffering from depression. He told me that what scares him the most, is helₗ ness, a completely dark hole he's falling into. He was lying on a couch, not very comfortable, but a comfortable-looking one, and I was looking at him.

"You are still listening to the wrong tune," I said.

Most people suffer from an unnamed disability syndrome, which can be given a working description of a belief in their own uniqueness. We read in many self-help books for improving the well-being, that we should cultivate such conviction of the patients. It could not be more wrong. In their overwhelming majority, people are similar to each other. And that's my excuse to myself when I repeat the same statements to them, brazenly using the methodology referred to as "copy-paste".

"Do you know that I am friends with a well-known composer?" I continued. Then I told him about the soundtrack of a movie. And at the end I offered sheets of paper adorned with the logo of the clinic.

"But what is this treatment?" The man is clearly hesitating.

"It's an experimental therapy. I would like you to meet a certain young woman..."

Yes, I realize that pimping is a rather strange method of treating a depression. What the hell! The girl's name was Berenice, but she did not have a braid*, which is not obligatory nowadays, although her parents were undoubtedly dissatisfied... My assistant has a face of a woman, which I can't even describe. Sometimes, especially

---

* Coma Berenices, in Polish Berenice's Braid

when logic fails, the mind is filled with bubbling emotions - the light ceases to be an orderly set of particles, and becomes a wave. It is not about the fact that she was infinitely beautiful - her nose would not send a thousand ships into the sea, and the features were lacking in classic symmetry. But even the analytical brain of a man in his prime shudders at the statement that beauty is only a kind of geometry. Rather, it is something silent, unspecified - a mirage melting in the morning mist, a dance of changing sun rays on the leaves (or maybe only on the retina?), a feeling of complementing the opposites that mysteriously protects the garden gate against the intrusion of the chaotic world.

"So how are you now, after few meetings with Berenice?" I asked him the next Wednesday.

"Doctor..." The man could hardly say a word. "It was amazing, from the very beginning, from the moment she spoke to me. At that time I understood with absolute certainty, with some pornographic literalness, that it was her voice that I had been waiting for my whole life."

"What did she tell you?"

The patient smiled.

"Nothing special." He replied. "I guess "hi, fatty"... And in this greeting I heard the potential for future conversations in the morning, in an empty tavern on the sea side, in the unconscious company of pirates sleeping in a drunken sleep, or maybe this never-happened meeting will take place in medieval libraries, or on a spaceship speeding into faster-than-light skies?"

"And that's what I wish for you," I answered cheerfully. "Today you pay only two hundred zlotys. I'll see you in a week."

* * *

I can't explain this falling into self-irony, into bizarre mental pirouettes and showmanship. As if I suddenly could not separate this pathetic efflorescence of the imagination from the real world, as if I tried to blur the reality in impropriety, instead of describing it with the appropriate words. I have often wondered recently if I am losing my mind myself. And on top of that, those damned Black Harpists.

Of course, I will not reveal to the police or anyone else, how I get my knowledge about these beings. If I admitted that I had heard this story from a guy living on the ceiling, I would definitely go back to the psychiatric facility, but this time as a patient. As F. Scott Fitzgerald said, no fire, no immaculate glow of purity matches what a man can carry in the depths of his haunted heart. I would add that even the monsters living in the ceilings and partition walls are not able to match this.

It so happened that the ceiling looked at me and apparently decided that as a psychiatrist, I had to be a good listener. How fascinating this story was, perfectly suspenseful, abounding in extraordinary protagonists and sudden twists. Well, the storyteller certainly guaranteed an amazing experience, right? However, with all due respect for the inhabitant of my plafon, I could not blab far and wide what I learned from him. That's why I told the policemen so little. I had to reveal a little more to the Majewski family, but I still kept some details for myself. Besides, the guy from the chandelier asked me quite firmly to do so, and I did not want to upset him.

***

First of all, I did not tell anyone about the war between the Harpists representing different colors. If the issue of this conflict came to light, which posed a risk of the collapse of the universe, no less, the whole country would panic. In fact, it turned out that the Black Harpists, guarding human dreams, fight the White Harpists, who bring the worst nightmares. I thought about Majewski. They did not realize that their problem is far beyond what has happened to them so far. For now, they were plagued by nightmares, but madness awaited them as soon as the thin border between the worlds would burst, and the sleepy matter would spread in our reality. I have experienced firsthand the merciless effects of insanity many times, of this violent manifestation of the unconscious, ripped out, thrown up in sudden paroxysms into the light of day. I was a doctor of human souls after all. A harpist of the real world, not endowed with as much as a trace of music ear.

***

Today I am going to a city dressed as a woman again. You think you can penetrate my mind, so you can judge me and my emotional life with no doubt? Eh, you do not understand. It's just a camouflage so that I do not need to reveal to the world my true nakedness, my dark secret.

And above all, my curse is the similarity to the politician of the ruling party, because of which I can't count on even a little privacy. When you see a guy in women's clothes, probably a disgusting pervert, then you do not want to pay too much attention to him to not get infected with his perversion, so that others would not see an even more sick perversion in you.

I will visit a few bars for singles tonight, perhaps I will learn more about the Harpists. This is my current obsession, my passion, from which I can't free myself. But it's hardly surprising if you know a little bit about the subject. But that's enough, I do not have to stroke your genetically modified brains with some kind of bloated descriptions of nature, or eyewitness truth. I must be honest with the world in which I live, and you are not this world at all. And that's it.

I used to think that returns are mathematically impossible, because all places are constantly changing. That the space from which we left is already in completely different place when we return. There was not a hint of originality in these statements, which I admit with humility, appropriate to my age. Today, however, I know how wrong I was, and it does not give me the slightest satisfaction. I read on the wall of a public toilet, that the belated truth is worse than a premature lie. I do not glorify "toilet poetry" at all, but from a medical point of view, I admit that it helps people to defecate. But even this poetry does not explain my fascination with Harpists.

We can't leave, because the place where we are, moves with us.

∗∗∗

The observer is experiencing a revelation. He already knows how he can help the Majewski. However, he has no idea if he will be able to pass them the solution to the problem. Maybe sometimes the words themselves are enough, their right choice, the right time of their delivery. So he could send a letter to them... Oh, of course, it would be too easy from the dramaturgy point of view. Besides, another breach of the border between the worlds could have tragic consequences. Maybe he could send an animal that would pass the message? Except the talking dogs arouse great public interest in that world, or at best they become the heroes of bestsellers.

With a sense that the time is shrinking, the observer freezes thoughtfully somewhere between the cinderblocks and the layer of Styrofoam...

Chapter 8

MARC

Someone is watching us all the time, when we circulate - Martha and I - endlessly through this strange garden. The trees lift their branches - the vaults of the ancient catl ls of the dark gods. From the distance come the mysterious sounds resembling the singing of priests of an unknown, yet terrifying religion. One can feel the smell of mildew, and every now and then we recognize in morbidly bloated flowers the faces of the dead, coming alive for a blink of an eye and trying to get out. Oh! If only we could get out of these colorful frames, from the caricature of the world in which we were imprisoned! The worst, however, is the sense of the presence of a foreign mind, the creator of this orangery. A mind so superior to ours, that it must cause mad horror. We are looking around desperately. So many plants lying in wait for our misstep! Their stems are covered with a jelly-like substance that evokes distant associations with the walls of abandoned graves. The strands of vines are hanging above our heads like the hideous fingers of Yog-Sothoth. Martha grabs my hand and I try to cheer her up. The greenery surrounds us from every side, hiding these all-seeing eyes, from which there is no escape. We know, however, that we will find a portal somewhere near, and free ourselves from this trap. We have lost our maps irretrievably, but Martha swears that she remembers the scheme with the evacuation route marked on it. We also realize that the passage must be masked, that it does not resemble at all the familiar gate with an electronic panel behind a transparent glass. We scour the bushes more and more nervously, and hundreds of small creatures scoot from under our feet. Suddenly Martha smiles at me with a face that looks for a moment like belonging to a madman.

"See this glow?" - she asks, pointing to the tree and its roots, hugging a small hill in a loving embrace, as if they wanted to squeeze the corpse juices out of it. I look at my wife worryingly. It's just an old wild apple tree... But Martha is walking towards the tree, and a confidence unexpectedly shows in her movements, although it begins to rain and the whole world plunges into spasm of a fever. She has already climbed the hill and reaches for a fruit hanging heavily from a dead branch. After a while, she picks the apple and I too notice the light coming from the sky. The shadows spread in all directions, the apple tree disappears, and the fuzzy shape of a great gate begins to show where the branches were swaying a moment ago. "It is a portal!" - I shout in amazement. - "How did you know?" And she grins at me in a bizarre grimace, prattles something about the schema of an escape route, about a snake whose image adorned the legend of the lost map, and her fingers reach out greedily to mine. We leave the garden, follow the emptiness opening behind the gate, embraced and free.

***

It was surprising, but this dream brought me relief, as if I had found my way in the dark. Even the unsuccessful search in the libraries for any mention of Harpists was not able to change that. When I told Martha about the tree of knowledge, she smiled slightly.

"Oh dear, I don't know... Why did these gnostic topics come to your mind?"

"Oh, let's ignore all the ornaments," I said. "This dream carries the promise of solving our problems."

"I wish I had that much faith, my undaunted optimist."

I hugged her.

"Can I tell you something?"

She had to know that the moment of confessions came, because she nodded eagerly.

"A writer once said that our souls live in a dark forest and it is not easy for them to find the lit up paths. If this is really happening, then you are my clearing..."

She kissed me and I returned it immediately. And that was just the beginning.

***

The old woman was standing by the gate, and because she did not look like a Jehovah's Witness, I decided to go out to her. She looked like a typical representative of a group of "mohair berets"*, but there was a mysterious depth in her gaze.

"Can I help you?"

And then she opened her mouth, from which came whistles most similar to dolphin speech. I felt pure fear overwhelm me. The old woman whistled, staring stubbornly at my eyes. She also started waving her hands in a bizarre pantomime.

"Please, ma'am..," I tried to stop her, but my attempts failed. The woman emitted a couple more of the loud sounds, waved her hands violently, then turned back and sprinted down the street. Suddenly it got darker. It was as if the clouds were changing their structure and began to resemble the ruins of sky-high fortresses. I went back to Martha and told her about this whole weird episode. I must admit that my wife was very intrigued with it.

"Oh, honey... Maybe it was just an old crazy woman?" She wondered.

"Maybe she was a madwoman," I said. "It still remains to be explained how she managed to make such strange noises."

"Remember that you.., both of us are stressed... Maybe this lady simply went crazy, I don't know... So her language seemed unintelligible to you?"

---

* the expression referring to the stereotype of elderly women who are catholic-nationalistic fanatics and often wear mohair berets

I nodded. Perhaps one had to look at the whole event with the cool eye of a scientist. Soon, however, we found out that the world around us was going crazy. Dreams were crawling out of the darkness of the night, blindfolded, as the dreams usually are. As soon as they set the first, careful step on the canvas of the reality, nothing could stop them.

***

On the same day we had another peculiar visit. This time, the familiar policemen visited us. It did not surprise us that they took on acting roles, and their inspiration were the lead characters of the movie Lethal Weapon.

"Do you use drugs?" Śmigielski asked quite unceremoniously.

"What a nonsense idea," I said sharply. The absurdity of this question hung in the air like a miniature, invisible zeppelin.

"Are you sure?" The Assistant Commissioner continued. "No weed, or maybe a little ecstasy on hot, Saturday nights?"

"You insult us with these questions. After all, we have small children," Martha joined in.

"Maybe you just sell them, no?" Sabol suggested in an insolent tone. Thus, the concept of the "good cop, bad cop" scenario fell apart in front of our eyes.

"Easy, easy," I interrupted. "You don't have any evidence for your, completely fabricated, theory. My only contact with drugs was in college. My friend offered me some 'weed'" and it did not have any effect anyway. And that's all."

"You understand that we're investigating a murder. We do not ask these questions to carry on a nice conversation over coffee..." said Śmigielski.

Theoretically, he was right. However, the manner of conducting this interrogation really annoyed me. As if we had no other reason to worry! Both policemen pretended to be Roger Mutaugh and

Martin Riggs for another moment, then said goodbye to us. What a couple!

***

The visit of a strange old woman and equally bizarre policemen made us quite worried. We realized then that it could not go on like this anymore, and that it was time to take some steps. It was probably then that we understood one more thing - life is something more than just a line of breaths, a long route measured by heartbeats. It got through to us, as Robert Musil once wrote, that there are periods in which life clearly slows down, as if hesitating, whether to move forward or change direction. Perhaps it is in such periods that a disaster happens more easily. When I repeated this quote to Martha, she stated that it is just the opposite - our life suddenly accelerated. Either way - that day we were at the top of the mountain, from which distant horizons could be seen, but the path to them remained hidden. Martha declared that she would search on the Internet and in the library next day, and meanwhile I would talk to Alfred Albiński, our librarian friend. However, we still had to survive another night, face the new nightmares crawling out from between the walls.

***

This time, I dreamed about the Black Harpists themselves. This place reminded a philharmonic hall, although it was not it at all. Maybe it was because of the festive outfits of the guests gathered in the audience, and perhaps the monumentality of the granite walls; in any case, I saw a dozen or so ape-men on the stage, armed with Celtic harps, who made melancholic sounds based on a grim minor-key scale. At some point, the music sounded louder, and bloody scraps and identifiable fragments of human bodies began to fall down from the precipice rising above the heads. It was as if I was under a giant meat grinder, although maybe it was a completely prosaic precipitation in this strange land? Then, out of nowhere, owls appeared, catching this unusual manna from heaven in their claws. Have you noticed that some species of owls look like birds from other planets? That was exactly my thought in this dream.

Suddenly, the music started to fade and after a while, the nightmarish musicians began to put away their instruments inside black covers. The owls were long gone, earlier the night birds had perfectly cleaned the whole surface I could see from the blood and human remains. I had the impression that the Harpists began to hurry, as if they were trying to escape those who would come here in a moment. I also wanted to get out of there, from this room, from this dream, from this world. But I didn't know how to close my eyes in order to wake up.

***

"I have never heard this story before," Alfred admitted after a long silence. My friend was without doubt the most well-read man I knew. If he could not help me, then the things looked hopeless.

"So the matter looks hopeless?" I asked, without even expecting the confirmation of my thoughts.

"Oh, I wouldn't draw such far-reaching conclusions... We can use, for example, the SLN resources."

It turned out that SLN is an acronym for the Secret Library Network.

At a time when our every step in the virtual world is being followed, and even the super-secret TOR network begins to be infiltrated, people have turned to the past. Towards a small library collection, hidden where they are most difficult to find, to reading rooms for the chosen, where you could read in peace the book not accessible anywhere else.

"How far is the nearest reading room like this" I wanted to know.

"Very close. In the neighborhood club for muscle-men."

Right, it was quite a logical answer. Later, Alfred told me that one day he listened to a conversation of two young men with beautiful muscles, bald skulls and tasteful sports suits with three stripes. It turned out that they were discussing a little-known Catalonian writer who recently published a new collection of short stories. My friend was most surprised by the passion with which both fans of steroid desserts discussed literature. As he stated in the summary of this anecdote, the secret library will soon have to be moved into a more discreet place, since the sweatshirts cease to be a confusing element. For me, the whole story had a reassuring effect, because it showed people are still able to surprise us in a positive way.

But, the two of us were going to the reading room - what an emotional event! I still hoped that we would find information there, which would help us unravel the mystery of the Black Harpists. However, at some point, a sudden thought appeared in my head. I began to wonder if the madness flowing out of the nightmares is not slowly soaking into our reality. That old woman trying to tell me something in the language of dolphins, the strange behavior of the psychiatrist, eh... Even the police officers were not quite normal. It all began to resemble a scenario of a dream.

Down the stairs to the basement, then a long corridor dimly lit with old fluorescent lamps. We were in the Pumping Iron Gym, as the inscription on the front door happily announced. We hurried past two young men on elliptical machines, navigating between the bars and atlases covered with sweat. Alfred led me to the next door - this time with the sign "Authorized personnel only". And again we found ourselves in the corridor. It was much darker here than in the previous rooms. My companion suddenly opened a door and we were at our destination. A rather surprising view appeared to my eyes. The great hall was full of columns filled with books. Among these round bookshelves stood desks with small lamps. There were not many people, maybe they were hidden somewhere in the arcades. We approached an old-fashioned catalog.

"Let's search under 'harpists'. We need to look through it carefully. Surely we will have to filter out a lot of information about Turloch O'Carolan or Nicanor Zabaleta, but we may get lucky." Alfred's voice sounded rather optimistic. I also felt good about it.

Indeed, most of the entries in the catalog were personal. We had long hours of searching ahead of us. While reading volume after volume of mossy books, I learned more and more about the instrument itself. It turned out, for example, that the harp was already known in Asia Minor about five thousand years ago. It appeared also in an ancient culture of Mesopotamia (sources mention the so-called harp of Ur). There is also a proverb from the tenth century, which mentions three things necessary for happiness: 'a faithful wife, a comfortable chair and a well-tuned harp'. Interestingly, harp-like instruments can be found in many cultures. For example, the Chinese stringed instrument called konghou is very similar to it. Perhaps it happened that the harp was an object from a different reality, and thus it has long imprinted its mark on archetypical musical solutions. Nowhere, however, could we find information about the Black Harpists. At some point, I was overcome with premature joy when I came across an article about the Coalition of Harpists of African Descent. Alfred was much more lucky - he found a nineteenth-century monograph on the history of harpists, in which an entire chapter was devoted to myths and legends. It mentioned a certain ancient work called the Codex Sygmanta de Syntagmum, which was supposed to contain instructions for people who want to physically enter the Land of Dreams. We were on the right track.

"I'll search the secret library catalogs," Alfred said happily.

We soon found out that one copy of the work mentioned can be found in Radom. To tell the truth, it was the last place where I would look for this type of knowledge, but I was slowly beginning to understand that the reality ceased to be guided by rational premises. We were therefore going to make a trip to this city, which some still called the Milan of the North. I just hoped that the world around me would calm down a bit. Of course, the hope was dashed.

SOMEONE ELSE IS DREAMING IV

I love novels for teenagers, now known under the code name young adult. It kind of explains my dream last night.

This is another love story, like many others, but this fact can't stop me from telling it. Because there is no justification for silence - even when the convenience tells us to lock all the stories in the dungeons under the palace. When the birds shout in the morning and you hear the sound of a million feet sentenced to exile, and the scream of mermaids pushes the ship to the rocks, one can't be silent.

***

Maria came from a distant planetary system. She was never willing to reveal its name. "It's two, maybe three thousand light years away," she said. I thought then that the distance does not exist. I remember telling Maria that even a weak thread would lead me to her through the abyss of the universe. Today I know that the labyrinths of stars are more extensive than I thought, but this will not stop me from going for further search.

We met for the first time at the space port. It was a December morning. In the crowd of arrivals, she stood out not only in height. Her blue hair waved to the rhythm of her steps ("How do you do it that the light always dances in your hair?"). The angel wings only emphasized the perfect line of her back. When she stopped and looked around the waiting people, her eyes quickly caught the screen with the company logo floating over me ("How do you do it that the light always dances in your eyes?").

"You're from the Virtue Company, right?" She asked. "Maria de Mea."

I bowed my head in a ritual greeting.

"Kalten Yevs, president of Virtue, how are you."

The way she looked at me made it difficult to maintain the correct angle of my neck.

"Can we go now? I'm quite tired after the trip..."

Her mocking eyes suggested that she knew very well what effect she had on me.

So we got into the mobil. After all, you can't argue with a representative of the Masters race.

***

The Celestians appeared on Earth two hundred years ago. Ever since my childhood, I have been wondering about their phenomenon - how did they manage to subdue people so quickly. I think we were doomed to this fate from the beginning. Can you resist angels? We had this archetype firmly imprinted after all - like the Incas. It was the memory of the Viking ships that sentenced them to death at the hands of the conquistadores. We were in the same situation.

The Celestians were so reminiscent of the images of angels from the old paintings, that the civilization breakthrough that occurred after their arrival to Earth can be easily explained. Sociologists agreed that the recognition of strangers as the embodiment of beauty and sanctity had condemned us to this apparent loss of independence, because the human race likes to put the beings that can be worshiped on a pedestal. Today, we do not believe in angels or gods anymore, because we think that the fate of humanity is written in The Carpet, but when we look at a beautiful, winged woman with blue hair, we are overwhelmed by an atavistic longing, a whining of a forgotten puppy who became an adult dog many years ago.

***

We drove in silence, and the turbines of the power plants we were passing whirled outside the windows, driven by unyielding winds. Maria was looking at me quizzically.

"Do you believe in destiny?" She asked suddenly.

I looked in the rearview mirror, trying in vain to guess the context of the question.

"On Earth, we think that the fate is ruled by The Weaver, who weaves individual threads into The Carpet's tapestry. We do not give her the divine traits, but we personify Fatum in this way."

The Celestian laughed softly.

"Do you believe in angels?"

"It's not a matter of faith but of perception," I replied. "We stop believing in something that we saw with our own eyes."

Maria slightly cocked her angelic neck.

"I see that you are not a stranger to courtesy..."

"It's not courtesy, it's honesty," I laughed nervously.

"In that case I will give you more opportunities for it," she smiled ("How do you do it, that the light is always dancing on your face?").

"I hope I will not disappoint you, madam."

"Maria."

-"Kalten."

And that's how it started.

***

At first, our relations were purely professional. The Virtue company, of which I was the president, prepared spatial advertising sculptures, which later scared those traveling through the asteroid belt, emerging like rocky specters pursuing the cosmic ships. Maria came to oversee the work on a new series of sculptures for the Intergalactic Hairdressing Consortium. So I was the head of my company only nominally, the ordinances flowed from the cosmic emptiness in a stream of data, and now Maria also appeared as an incarnation of the race ruling over us.

Gradually, however, a misty shadow of familiarity began to creep in between us. It grew out not only of my rather obvious infatuation. I want to say that even though I let my imagination loose, I would not have gone beyond the world of fantasy without Maria's approval. Anyway, in fact she was the one who took the first step. It could be expected, after all, this is the scenario written by the story of our two races. The initiative always comes from the stronger side.

***

The panocean coast in June resembles deserted ruins of a destroyed city. Tourists choose the warmer and more crowded south, while ragged cliffs weave with nostalgia their long tale of loneliness. We got here, however, because after completing the order and sending the manicured sculptures into space, Maria wished a get away from the city. She said that the coastal landscapes remind her of the scenery of her native world, whose name she did not want to give me.

We sat on the terrace, and there was only a bored waiter, dressed as a giraffe, lingering near us. Sipping martinis, we discussed work and life. Billions of similar conversations hung over us in the form of invisible festoons.

"You know Kalten, what I just thought of?" Maria said suddenly.

My face turned into a question mark.

-"I came to the conclusion that angels need people more than vice versa. If no one is worshiping you, you are only an object, a disembodied voice in the abyss of heaven. It is only when someone loves you that you become a divine being."

I looked into her eyes, which were, as always, a dance of flames.

"A burnt offering as food for the angel's soul?"

Maria laughed, and her laughter caused a shiver on my back, as usual.

"I would like to become an angel - she said softly, and her hand magically met my hand."

I looked at her dancing light and after a while I became a part of it. Our kiss must have been visible to astronomers on distant planets.

We ran upstairs, throwing off clothes along the way.

***

When she was lying in my arms like a tired bird, I stroked her wings and re-experienced the events of the last night, again and again. Daybreak crept quietly behind the windows, like a cat hunting for a mouse. Her fluorescent body slowly regained its true color. Suddenly Maria woke up and turned her face to me.

"You know I will not stay here forever?" She asked with a worry in her eyes.

"I know, I know..." I replied absently.

We lay for a long time, staring at the clouds rolling over the horizon. All the time in the world concentrated in a single moment. In silence, thundering from unspoken words, we began again.

And then... The days passed in a crazy dance. When she looked at the stars, I knew she missed home. On July nights, she looked up more and more often, and I could not stop the fleeing minutes. I sensed then that I could keep her with me with one word, erase the longing from my heart and hobble her will forever. However, I remained silent.

And then August arrived.

***

As usual at this time of year, the meteor shower came. We stood on the rock terrace, holding hands. The ocean boomed below, but it did not make any impression on the granite rocks of the coast.

"I would like to be a night, so that I could look at you with my thousand eyes," I said quietly.

I like to draw from the treasury of aphorisms, because I know that my own words will never reach the horizon. I looked into her eyes, but suddenly, the sky exploded with the rain of stars. Maria touched my face.

"It's really funny... People think that saying a wish while seeing a falling star guarantees it will come true. While in fact, it is exactly the opposite..." she said.

"How come?"

"It is the power of human words, whispered at the right moment, that throws the stars off the sky. You just have to hit this one fraction of a second, written in the firmament chronicles," she turned toward the sea.

I know what she wanted to tell me. That's when I realized that it is exactly the same with love. The most impassioned confession of one's feelings, told at dawn in the light of the rising sun, will not be met with a response if it is not the right dawn and the right sunlight. However, I understood it too late. The spirit of the stairs caught with me again.

***

We were standing in the parking lot, and the river was singing below. The peaks of the surrounding mountains did not pay attention to the asphalt road thrown into their shadows by ancient builders. It was late afternoon.

"It's time for me. Take me to the spaceport," she said, her face expressing a deep confidence that the decision she had just made was right.

I looked at Maria in silence. After a while, we got into the mobil and went on the road. The song of the river rose above the valley and fell, according to the eternal score.

***

When her cosmic chariot disappeared in the sky, I was devastated. I have irretrievably lost the love of my life, the angel who came down to earth to love a mortal. I returned to the empty house, staring blankly at the gray walls. I did not know the name of her planetary system, and the whole universe was scattered with millions of worlds inhabited by Celestians. I felt fooled by the brightness of the setting sun and the birdsong rising somewhere thousands of meters above the city.

And it was like this for many days. I got drunk unconscious before bedtime, to wake up in the morning, after a dozen or so seconds, with a monster hangover. The company has not yet received any new orders, so there was nothing that could distract my despair. One morning, however, among the vapors of alcohol bubbling under my skull, I felt a strange shiver on my back. I could not see anything worrisome in the bathroom mirror (except my drunken face of course). The next day, the chills ran up my spine again. I went to the doctor.

***

"You have wings sprouting on your back," said Dr. Fraud. I'll be damned!

And I already knew that it was a farewell gift from Maria. But I also felt a surge of unexpected optimism.

"What are you so happy about? It's some kind of a mutation. It might metastasize," said the doctor.

However, my face was lightened with an even wider smile. A man is not able to find an angel after all. But an angel will easily find a man.

***

I've been looking for you all over the universe for five years. Soon I will come across your trail. I know that the threads of the same fabric are not always intertwined. It all depends on the whims of The

Weaving, who only occasionally sees the image of the whole Carpet. Usually, however, she creates weaves spontaneously, without pity for the lost patterns. But I know that I will find you in the mazes of the stars.

Chapter 9

ŚMIGIELSKI

My boss was getting more and more weird, I concluded at nine o'clock on that day when we were to interrogate Bison. The uncrowned king of the nei... sub-world did not want to testify without a lawyer, which meant another pain in the ass. In addition, Sabol was losing his marbles, that was the way to describe it. I know, I also wanted to become an actor someday, but I said goodbye to this dream. Doesn't the maturity mean letting the dreams of youth go? Sure, it's nice to have a role to play sometimes, because "when the actor doesn't have a role, he doesn't know why to live, why to eat"*... Except that then come the loans, debits on the accounts, unpaid bills, and wild teenagers demanding their ransom of pocket money. You'll probably ask me what I'm doing in the Police in that case. Or maybe whether the rumors of a low pay in uniformed services are not exaggerated by any chance? I have my reasons - I will retire at the age of forty-something, and maybe then I will find time to pursue my plans. For now, we play in one team, all hands on deck and long live the justice, ha ha.

At today's hearing, Sabol was supposed to be the Terminator, or an android type T-800, played by the governor Schwarzenegger in the original version. I was thus left with the role of a second, more communicative cop. I must admit that my supervisor was simply born to play the "electronic killer", as the original title from the eighties of the twentieth century was charmingly translated. However, his exterior could and did deceive many a criminal, who

---

* A song by Jacek Kaczmarski

did not have pleasure to meet Sabol before. But Bison was not one of them.

Before entering the interrogation room, Sabol put on dark glasses. We were ready.

As usual, Bison dressed up in an expensive tailored suit, but it was tailored for somebody else. Other than that, it was all standard - gelled hair in the style of the early Presley, a fashionable hipster beard, glasses in delicate frames, a tasteful cane with inlaid head. A golden Rolex on his wrist complemented the look. His lawyer's face, on the other hand, wasn't like anything to look at.

"What do you want this time, doggies*?"

I noticed Sabol clenching his jaws angrily, so I quickly took the initiative.

"Easy, Bison, or your hair may get tousled. Our sources have provided information about the death of one of your soldiers..."

"As they say, a la guerre comme a la guerre. Of course, I have no idea what you're talking to me about, doggie."

"Shut up, you trash, no, and listen!" The Commissioner lost his temper. "We know everything. About the drug war, about the new stash in the city, about your connections. And a murder remains a murder, even if it is just some weed you pulled out!"

"You calm down," Bison retorted. "I know you have nothing on me, but you may have information that I would like to trade in a barter. What is this murder?"

I looked at Sabol. He nodded almost imperceptibly.

"First tell us something about this new stash," I said.

Bison consulted with his lawyer for a moment, then he smiled under his breath.

"I will share gossip with you, dogs. Well, the rumor has it that a completely new kind of drug has hit the market. Apparently it has

---

* A contemptuous slang name for policemen.

very unusual effects. The junkies move, literally, not figuratively, into a colorful world, each time to the same one. You understand? It's like Narnia, but without all the fuss with the wardrobe, or Hogwart without the bothersome search for the platform nine and three-quarters. Apparently, they even call this new stuff the London-Hogwart Express. But I only repeat what I have heard. This might be just a mambo-jumbo invented by a stoned addict."

"And you have nothing to do with it, right?" Sabol chuckled.

"Scout's honor, dear dogs..."

"And do you happen to know how to get a sample of this stuff?"

"Well, I have some friends. But tell me now, what about this murder? Of course, I'm interested in this matter as a concerned citizen of our district."

I told him the story of a strange case from a dozen days ago, of course without going into details. Bison listened, and a very morose expression appeared on his face. He did not seem to like my story.

"It's very disturbing. So you say the body disappeared into thin air?"

"I did not use this expression," I protested.

"Maybe for the better, after all no one talks like that anymore. In a word, you do not have a corpse, you do not have evidence, just some hallucinations of this family?"

I had to admit he was right.

"So I would not care about it in your place, dogs."

"Shut up!" Sabol lost it again. "If you call us that again..."

"How should I call you then? Teddy bears, little bees or maybe butterflies?"

"That's enough." This time I cut it off. "Let's get to business. We might turn a blind eye to some of the reports, but you must provide us with a sample of this London-Hogwart express."

"I'll ask around among friends and let you know. Fine with me."

I felt that we achieved some agreement, albeit frail. And that's when Sabol started to go nuts.

"The machines rose from the ashes of the nuclear fire. Their war to exterminate mankind has raged for decades, but the final battle would not be fought in the future. It would be fought here, in our present."

Bison looked at me with a clear question in his eyes. Meanwhile, his lawyer was having a great time.

"Don't worry about him. We've got everything under control."

"You sure, dog?"

"Fuck you, asshole," Sabol recited.

Bison probably did not like such accurate movie quotes.

**

I brought coffee for the Commissioner and sat down against the wall. It was necessary to develop a strategy how to proceed.

"Did you notice that this brief hardly said anything at all?" I asked.

"Somehow I don't miss his brilliant comments, no? Shit, I'll be back!" Apparently, Sabol still could not get out of his role.

"Okay, calm down. What are we going to do with Bison?"

Sabol was looking at me from behind the dimmed glasses. At least I hoped so.

"We will get this drug, then we will take it, and we will follow the gang to the damned, Narnia, no?"

He definitely did not feel well. A sentence from a book came to my mind that its main character sometimes managed to believe in six impossible things already before breakfast. I would like to believe at least one.

"Come on Sabol, knock it off... You want us, the police officers on duty, to use illicit substances with unknown side effects?"

"We can go for a vacation for a moment, and then we'll come back from it."

Obviously, Sabol was convinced that his opinion about the case is the only right one.

"We will end up being fired and out on the street like some fucking Chopin's piano," I had to express my dissenting opinion at this moment.

"You knock it off, Śmigielski," he interrupted me. "You never really wanted to be transported to Wonderland, even as a child, no? As they say, it's a nice night for a walk!"

Further discussion seemed more and more pointless.

"What about our witnesses from Wietrzna Street? Are we coming back there?"

"If we do not receive another call, I would rather not show up at the crime scene again. It's better not to provoke Bison."

"So what are we doing now?" I wanted to know.

"We're going for lunch."

"Already? It is only noon."

-"John Connor, it's time!"

***

After lunch, the boss pulled himself together a bit and went to work at his desk. So I had a little time to think about all this. And above all - should I admit a certain insubordination to my superior?

Because here's what happened. Two days earlier I had a very strange evening visit. No, it was not a Gypsy that came to see me. This time it was an old acquaintance, back from the old time of child's horse plays in the backyard, Witold. We still met two or three times a year to reminisce about those days of glory. However, he rarely visited me, so something unsettling must have happened.

The old buddy asked for coffee, and when I returned to the room with two cups, he watched the graphics hanging on the wall. It showed a small grove full of trees that were cut in half from top to bottom. Smaller trees hid in their crowns.

"What is it?" Asked Witold.

105

"This is one of the pictures from a very strange book. Have you ever heard of Codex Seraphinianus?"

He shook his head.

"It was created by the Italian architect Luigi Serafini. This is a very specific encyclopedia of non-existent reality. It contains thousands of illustrations and it is written in an unknown language..."

"Something like the Voynich manuscript?" Apparently, my friend moved comfortable within this topic.

"Yes, something similar. But tell me, what brought you to me today?"

Witold stopped smiling. His story seemed devoid of any sense at first glance. For several days someone had been following him in the city. For some time it was a man dressed as a clown, then some old woman on a bike - he could have sworn that he saw her a few, if not a dozen times. A little later, a guy in a suit and dark glasses started following in his footsteps. When I asked Witold, why did he assume that it was the same guy, because after all there are a lot of suits around, he said that this supposed spy walked in a characteristic manner, stepping like a Japanese geisha. But this is not the end. Witold also received very peculiar telephone calls. The sound that came from the headphone resembled the noise of uploading software to an old eight-bit computers.

I was not sure how to help him, and I did not want to suggest a visit with a specialist too strongly. He left half an hour later, and it was only just before falling asleep that I remembered that my friend now lives on Wietrzna Street, so he is a neighbor of that suspicious couple from the disappearing body. Was it a coincidence? I do not think so.

But I was supposed to talk about the insubordination... I decided to investigate the Witold case myself, without involving Sabol in all this. I am not sure myself why I did it. We are friends after all, we used to appear together on theatrical stage, now we are serving in the Police. It would seem that he is the closest person to me, a soul mate, a twin brother found after many years. Except that he escaped to playing roles, and I helped him, probably mainly out of habit. For several years I have been suffering from clinical depression - of course, no one at the police station has any idea about it, not even Sabol. I swallow selective serotonin reuptake inhibitors, I go incognito to individual therapy. I even used to go to group meetings once, but it was too difficult an experience. In the end, I could not fully open in front of so many people, or feel a little better because of dropping the curtains of lies, when I was hiding behind the biggest lie, the lie of my identity. And to come back to Sabol - I felt that my superior and partner was starting to squelch me slightly, I wanted to finally owe something to myself. Maybe it's a bit of a silly excuse that probably would not stand up to a criticism from the internal department or even my boss, but hey, here it is.

Wietrzna Street seemed a quiet alley, like many others that can be found in the suburban area. The sidewalks are blocked by parking cars, even in the middle of the day, even though the houses look empty. I did not see too many walkers, maybe except for the scrappers sneaking from one property to another with their prams. And yet something else was hanging over the street, someone's inscrutable presence, like a quiet breath of wind on a hot day. I had the impression that I was being watched, although I probably would have known about such an eventuality. Years of practice, right?

But it is not always that simple. Sometimes all that one needs is a single furtive glance while on an empty bus, a laundry hung asymmetrically on a rope stretched between the trees, a painful pinch in the heart, when you read your favorite book after many years and realize that it simply astounds with its naivety and flat language. In such cases, you begin to understand - your existence is a collection of apparent elements that might just as well be arranged in a different order. So Wietrzna Street looked like a quiet alley, but one could feel in one's bones that this calmness was a matter of convention.

I carefully watched the windows of the houses I passed by, hoping to see a slight movement of curtains, someone's face stuck to the glass. But the buildings looked deserted, thujas and bougainvillea grew luxuriantly in the gardens, and clouds were slowly rolling in the sky. And it was in such a dead moment that I saw a man with a kayak.

Do you see the absurdity of this scene? I also felt then as if I was starting to go crazy, as if a mysterious, external force was manipulating the reality, or maybe just my perception of it?

I remember that I even began to wonder whether I had accidentally forgotten to swallow my morning dose of medication. It happened to me once and I was hallucinating then. Well, I'm not completely normal and I hope my work colleagues will never find out about it.

A man with a kayak was walking on the other side of the street, now hidden in the shadow, perhaps swept by wind from distant planets. I said that he was walking, though he was rather treading gracefully, balancing his floating unit and an oar, and looking around curiously. I approached him and he looked at me as if I was the first person he met today.

"Si estamos en Radom?" He asked.

"No, keinen Radom. Varsovie..." I answered a little uncertainly.

"Participo en un viaje en canoa, tuve que nadar por esta calle hasta Radom," he continued in his language, which I did not understand at all.

"Do you speak English?" I asked hesitantly.

"Lo sentimos, no hablo Ingles," he replied and nodded his goodbye. I stared at him for a moment with consternation, and then

I got into the car. I wondered if I still had anything to mention to Sabol.

And then I thought that I would be glad to talk to him about the book I just read, from which I cautiously noted one quote:

But why do we deal with this nothingness? Nothingness is rejected by science and sanctified as unreal. Science does not want to know anything about this "nothing". What is nothingness? Does nothingness exist only because there is a "no", i.e. a negation? Or maybe "no" and negation exist only because nothingness exists? We think: nothingness is a simple negation of the whole of being. Fear reveals nothingness. Nothingness nothingnesses itself.

Chapter 10

KALLEN

Daddy went somewhere, so I had to go to my mom. It's weird, because usually when our dad is home, the usual question me and my sister have for him is "Where is mo   l yet, now I'd rather talk about it with a boy. I wasn't sure myself why.

Mom was sitting in her favorite chair and reading some old newspapers. I went to her and smiled.

"Mom, I have a question..."

"Tell me, darling."

"Why do the trees make faces to me?"

She looked at me somehow strangely.

"What do you mean, Kallen?"

So I explained it to her. That I always found faces in tree trunks and between leaves, but now there were many more of them. And that it used to be normal faces like those of my friends or adults seen in the store or on the street, but that for some time they all had been becoming a bit hideous. As if they were making faces to scare me.

My mother always thought I had a fertile imagination. I guess so it was also this time, because she looked at me with the gaze that she usually used in similar moments. But I know when I just imagine something, or when I'm playing too hard and then I lose touch with reality, as a guy in the movie about Minecraft once said. It is different, however, when I see something Real. I'd really like to talk to my dad now, though I'm not sure it would be easier to explain to him what I saw.

"Don't worry, son. Me and your dad will protect you from evil creatures in the trees."

"Okay, mom, thanks."

"What is your sister up to?" She changed the subject.

I wondered for a moment what she was doing last time I saw her.

"I think she is swinging the spirits on the swing."

And then mom got really worried.

* * *

I see a lot of bizarre things lately, but it may have something to do with growing up. Well, because the adult world seems to me much more twisted from the world of children. Sometimes I listen to my parents' conversations at breakfast and I hardly understand anything. I can catch the general sense, I borrow some sentences for later, but I can't say that everything is clear to me, although I really like using words that I do not quite understand. It's like some of King Julian's talk. It's funny exactly because I do not get it completely.

The faces appear not only in the trees. I also see them in puddles, in the arrangement of shadows on the path I run when chasing my sister, in the most remote corners of the mirror I look into. I will say something funny now - one time a LEGO Star Wars man smiled funny me, I guess it was Han Solo, but I'm not sure now.

I also keep hearing unknown songs. Most often they come from behind the wall, but after some time I get the impression that someone plays them in my head. I know that this is complete nonsense, because how could someone in my head turn on an mp3 recording, similar to the one daddy sometimes listens to on the computer? Although I once heard on TV that our brains resemble large computers, so maybe there is Something Real in these voices? In any case, these songs are really amazing and they do not resemble the music that parents sometimes listen to. And I must say that my dad plays very bizarre bands sometimes.

I was talking about faces and songs. In addition, I always have the impression that someone is watching me - just like in the house where we were on vacation. Only there it was just video cameras, and I liked to fool around in front of them, jumping and dancing, staring at the still eye in the upper corner of the corridor. And now I do not feel like playing somehow.

My mum and I are going to the garden. She will probably want to hear something about this new play of Sophie. Eh, girls sometimes make up terribly stupid things. Today she came to me and said that her swing was visited by ghosts and she must now swing them, otherwise they would do something bad to all of us. She was just telling her story to mom, who did not seem to like what she heard.

"But Sophie, when did these ghosts talk to you?"

"I won't tell..."

"Honey, you promised recently that you would tell us everything."

Sophie was on the verge of crying.

"Yesterday before falling asleep, when I was listening to lullabies."

Mom hugged my sister.

"How did it happen? Tell me, sweetie."

Sophie began to talk. Apparently, the ghosts had been coming to her for some time. At first, they only offered her various games, but gradually began to demand all kind of strange things - arranging the crayons on a desk in a specific shape, singing a song in the bathroom, and now this swinging. I do not know what mom thinks, but in my opinion, Sophie is simply stupid. I would never listen to any spirit. Well, girls always behave in such a, well, girlish way.

Our mom, however, is also a girl, and I think that's why she understood well what my sister meant. She got very pale and it was obvious she was nervous. Maybe she also talked to ghosts? I decided to let the girls talk without me, I was not necessary, especially that some urgent matters awaited me in my room. Lloyd Garmadon had to go somewhere with a fire truck, and Baymax had to heal someone immediately. In addition, my geography atlas wasn't going to look through itself for the hundredth time this month.

And I had this strange impression again, as if someone pierced my back with his eyes. I turned around, but I only saw the two walls of the corridor, stained with blue, strangely empty, even though they must have been hiding the stranger's eyes of the cameras.

In my room I got busy with my LEGO blocks. I played with them on the floor and only after some time I sensed someone's presence. Girls probably chatted about ghosts or something else, the wind lightly tapped on the windows with the tree branches, and Lloyd Garmadon's friends tried to save a burning building. Then came this funny feeling - as if the wall was looking at me. I stared at it and it seemed to me that I could see the contours of a face. Kind of a white mask, looking like an old sculpture that I saw in a book. Pale, motionless, looking at me with empty eyes without pupils. I got scared.

And then I saw the second face emerging next to the first one, showing through the pattern of the wallpaper. This time the mask was black as ink, unimaginably ugly, but nevertheless it aroused only friendly feelings. First of all, it emanated some inner peace that made me feel safe. The white face contorted in a painful grimace and disappeared. Then the dark shape also blurred in the plant ornament on the wall. I hurried to the garden again, where mom was still talking to Sophie.

"You know, Mom, Suzie also had such common thoughts with ghosts once... She told me that they talked to her as if in her head. They told her fairy tales, sang songs, and went to kindergarten with her."

"And what happened next?" Mommy wanted to know.

"Nothing. Suddenly they stopped talking to her. Suzie said the ghosts got pouty and they went away."

"You have to listen to me very carefully now, my daughter. Spirits do not exist. Those voices that we hear in our head are only our own thoughts. Mind is playing with us in this way, makes us think we're talking to someone, but it's not a real conversation like now, when I talk to you, and Kallen is listening."

"How come, mom?"

"Sometimes our thoughts are so clever that they can convince us that they are not ours at all. And let me tell you that it works in the opposite direction, too. You can be convinced that you invented something yourself, while in fact you had heard this thing a long time ago and you just forgot about it."

"But, Mom..." I had to interrupt. "After all, the brain is like a big computer, and the computers themselves do not have intelligence. So how can it play with us as if we were strangers to it? It should listen to us, right?"

"You're right, Kallen. The problem is that this is not always the case."

"Can the brain make me see faces in a tree or in a wall?"

Mom hugged me.

"It does so very often, son. This even has a name, it is called an optical illusion."

Perhaps this was what was happening, and my mother told the truth. I will say even more - when our conversation ended, I was convinced that this was the case. But at night, when another nightmare came, I was not so sure about it anymore.

SOMEONE ELSE DREAMS V

I am afraid of falling asleep, that when I lose consciousness, he will come out from under the bed. For now I am lying with my eyes closed, making sure that no part of my body sticks out from under the quilt. I'm seven years old already, I have to be a grown up woman.

I am a mannequin left to my fate in an abandoned props storage room. Sometimes, a wind breeze, or a ray of sun that brings out color and texture in objects, gets inside through the closed windows. I can't go to meet this orgy of colors, I do not get to dance in the wind and waive my artificial hair to the rhythm of the white music. My legs, disconnected from the body, rest somewhere in the forgotten corner of the labyrinth like broken wings. I also do not have one hand - I like to think that because of it, I remind Venus of Milo. But I am far from vanity - even the carnival mask that I wear on my face proves it... Or maybe my disguise, this element of camouflage, is actually the sign of megalomania? Maybe I am waiting for someone who will tear off the veil and see the real face of the mannequin under the layers of disguise, but this view will not make him shudder with disgust?

Sometimes my friends visit me - broken toys and mechanisms thrown to the trash. How similar they are to me! This is one of the necessary features of friendship anyway... There is an artificial nightingale among them, who can't bring out any sound - how he suffers because of this... This music plays in him, he evokes a melody without any problems, but can't give it to anyone else anymore. An old jack-in-the-box with sad eyes and a long nose comes to see me almost every day, too. He repeats that he caught his owner lying and she could not forgive him for that. "It is the most difficult to forgive one's own sins" - I console him every time. I feel a close kinship with this old jack-in-the-box - he too has only one hand. Some make fun of him, but it's only because they have never seen him in the moonlight. Sometimes the teddy bear comes too, with sawdust insides that spill out from his belly.

I love their visits - the suddenly empty floors turn into endless dioramas of checkers, broken chairs become the kings' tombs, and all the moons flash outside the broken shutters. In those moments I have my legs again and I dance in a luminous circle, surrounded by a group of cats. When my friends leave, I'm just a broken mannequin again, an imitation of life. But I am sending the sad thoughts away, because I know that soon they will pay me a visit again...

***

Today came the jack-in-the-box, which infected me with an amazing idea. I am not able to grasp all the conclusions coming from this thought, it is too early for such reflections. For now, I let the mental reflexes circulate freely - let them echo in the cavities of the mind, like birds building nests above the abyss.

The jack-in-the-box believes that we create whole worlds in dreams, that it is only thanks to us that planets inhabited by billions of beings hang somewhere in the sky. Could our disability be only illusory, and the stumps - a play of an imagination, or the payment for a divine power? Can I wipe out whole armies with one impulse of my mind, or let the phantom finger of my nonexistent hand order the blossoming of billions of flowers? Today I will try to do it in my night's journey, what are these dreamed kingdoms for me? There are only inhospitable chasms stretching outside the window, which I could not get through, even if I had a pair of legs... And if I dreamed of this world, what will happen when I order to destroy it? I fall asleep with a light sleep that squashes me suddenly like a cold gravestone. I fall asleep in my store of props, failed works of creation. I fall asleep to not wake up.

And yet, I wake up, many of my nights are interrupted in this way... I have to go to the toilet. I make pee-pee and I'm going back to bed.

And again the ritual of hiding legs under a blanket, and then a bizarre dream.

Unraveling the mystery of the Lost N'Gai Tribe appears to me in the depths of memories like the unreal Mirrors Q'Lath. It brings to mind a distant land that I once visited in my dream, a scrap of a made-up biography. Does memory trick me and mock me cruelly when I fall asleep in an underground chamber? Or maybe these are obliterated brain pathways, lost connections of the synapses, or the spreading atrophy of the conductive mass?

In my youth I was a detective-historian. I researched the secrets of long-lost eons, I snatched them from the jealous tentacles of the God of the Past Days and inquired into the belated justice. In my profession, the solution to the riddle of the Lost N'Gai Tribe was an investigation of the investigations, the sweet promise of an oceanic wind, the culmination of the work. Many years later, a strange thought often haunts me - maybe I should not have reached for this discovery? Are not some truths treasured precisely because they are remote and unrealizable?

The lost N'Gai Tribe left little material evidence behind. Poorly preserved ruins of several cities on the hills surrounding the Trolls Bay, a few notes in chronicles of other tribes, snippets of old legends... Some of my academic colleagues even questioned the very existence of N'Gai, and thus treated the followers of this fascination with some contempt. However, I am the one who was right... I remember the mysterious box that appeared on the desk on that disastrous day. It contained an antique book and a letter from the director of a museum in the city of Qwlth. He stated in it, that he had found the trace of the Lost N'Gai Tribe, while looking through the archives of a certain family, given to him at the beginning of the timeperiod. He encouraged me to get acquainted with the find, while ensuring he was ready to offer all possible help in case I am interested. I jumped at the papers with the greediness worthy of a night predator.*

The documents sent to me by the helpful custodian suggested that the Lost N'Gai Tribe was banished to the desert that surrounded the city of Qwlth on three sides. Supposedly, the reason for this banishment was the disgusting cult that spread among N'Gaians. The records cited horrifying assumptions, told the story of the lost tribe that allegedly worshiped an ancient deity that came from the stars

---

* unusual word for the period of time, I guess meant to be an equivalent of the Earth's year

millions of years ago. These beliefs aroused such revulsion among the neighbors, that the N'Gai people had to settle among inhospitable sands far from civilization. According to the letter I received, the N'Gaians cultivated their faith in the gods from outer space also in exile. The director of the museum in Qwlth invited me to visit the excavation site near the settlement. I accepted this invitation with great joy.

The desert of Qwnqt greeted me with the monotonous singing of the wind wailing among the boulders, and the unnaturally pale blue of the sand, sifting into the rhythm of the dignified steps of the dunes. I reached the place of the find using a sled that a courteous museum worker let me use. There were several archeologists on site, who bowed to me with fear in their eyes, as if I were a ministry inspector.

Or maybe their fear had completely different basis? Now it's easier for me to judge that behavior, but maybe it's because I apply a filter of reminiscences, which haunt me in my underground chamber when I try to fall deeply asleep. I was unbelievably lucky - that was the day when the entrance to the N'Gaian temple was to be excavated.

***

I look at my notes and suddenly, like a bolt, comes an epiphany. After all, I was the one who discovered the secret of the Lost N'Gai Tribe! It was me who pored over the antique tomes and books to find the way to a city abandoned in the Qwnqtu desert! It was me who indicated the place where the excavations should begin! Where did this attempt to erase, falsify my memories come from? Am I so keen to deny my role? Or is it all a figment of a sick self who, in loneliness, adds glow to the long-forgotten glory? However, I will not change my notes - what is the authenticity of the days gone by, if nobody can verify it? The past never becomes the cabinet of wax figures, rather it is an aerial boat flying away in the wind, a sculpture losing contours in a poisonous rain.

Cold is my underground chamber, and the heat, escaping like a cloud, hovers among the stalactites, to never return.

* * *

I entered the dark cave with my heart in my mouth. The terrified scientists refused to accompany me, and this nice director of the museum escaped long ago in his sled. Every now and then, strange inscriptions appeared on the walls in the metallic light of the laser flashlight. The corridor led down at an angle of a dozen or so degrees, toward the voracious nucleus of the planet. In a moment I was going to see something that would change my life forever, a gloomy ghost haunting every dream, suddenly peering out of mirrors.

* * *

The tunnel suddenly changes into a huge room. I hear whispers of strange creatures inhabiting the interior of the rocks. There is a mysterious statue in the middle of the room. Ah! How terrible is this figure, wearing an iron dress... It has only two pairs of legs, one of which used for moving, and a hideous growth in the place of a head, its shape resembling a bubble... A pair of eyes looks at me from a bubble - just one - and the lips look like water snails known from oceanic walks... And then this bristle growing on the upper part of the head, which makes me want to throw up, and strange inscriptions on the body... This creature resembles arboreal mammals living in the jungles of the middle of the continent. It's a monkey in a shiny suit. The disgust makes all my tentacles tremble, venom drips uncontrollably from my fangs, and each head shakes in the sudden attack of repulsion... I'm not surprised that the N'Gai tribe has been banished - how can you worship such a repulsive being? It will haunt me in my dreams for hundreds of timeperiods, I will never forget this nightmare until the stony emptiness comes, and the good deities take me back to them. And if the gods are these strangers from the stars? Even death will not be an escape then. But it was my race that was

119

created in the image and likeness of the Supreme Being... Or maybe I'm wrong?

Chapter 11

Vinicius

How did it happen that I decided to climb the rope, hanging from the ceiling, to Skeleton Lake? What motivated me, what was the idea behind this seemingly poi erprise?

After all, as I said earlier to the policemen, the passage to the land of Harpists was in the wall of the Majewski's house, not in the ceiling of my apartment. And yet I found myself in a parallel universe, for which there is no difference, which removes all differences. It was bound to happen, it was clearly destined for me.

But I will start from the beginning, from my evening escapade along the trail of the night clubs, which I have traveled as Ligia Winnicka - yes, I know that the name of my female version was not strikingly original. The night was warm, as it is still possible in September, the marble walls of the buildings were dripping with light and glass, people on the streets seemed joyful. Yes, my city was slowly moving from Asia to Europe. I walked unhurriedly along the pavements, trying to make my hips sway rhythmically. It was a difficult trick, perhaps one of the hardest to master. Nobody accosted me, which I secretly deplored, but it would soon change. In one of the streets of the Old Town, three smoking guys with ironic smiles on their faces stood in my way. Once again, I cursed myself for insisting on growing a mustache. Because there are people who do not like women with mustaches.

"Hey, doll, where are you going?" I heard. "Got smokes?"

I shook my head helplessly. I started looking for a possible way to escape. Running around the Old Town pavement in high heels could end quite painfully, however.

"Got any dough on you?" Asked the other.

The situation was slowly getting quite ugly. Fortunately, I saw an approaching group of people. Men wore stylized and tight-fitting shirts of the cycling world champions, with rainbow stripes on their torsos. I was saved because I could of course easily recognize the famous Gaycommando in them.

"What is going on here? Are you accosting the lady, rascals?"

The three assailants moved at a distance away from me.

"We just wanted to mooch a smoke..." mumbled one of them.

"Don't you know smoking is bad for you?" The boss of the Gaycommando chuckled. "Well, get lost now, I don't want to see you here again."

The ruffians did not need another encouragement. They quickly disappeared somewhere around the old town square. The man in the cycling leotard looked at me.

"Where are you going, baby? Do you need an escort?"

I thanked politely and left for Miodowa.

The first meeting place awaited me there.

***

The Mad Hatter's bar was much more crowded than usual. I pushed my way to the table in the corner. A tall woman with a topper hat on her head was sitting there, in the company of silhouettes woven from a smoke. I smiled at her in a greeting.

"Verdana, how nice to see you!"

She tapped the ashes from her cigarette and looked at me over the lenses of her glasses.

"Oh, Ligia, great you are here."

Verdana was a copywriter at one of the leading agencies on the market. She believed once that ads can change people for the better, stimulate them intellectually, make them look at the world from a different, more interesting perspective. Of course, the ideals of youth are quickly deposited on the altar of comfort. I know that she now produced slogans about washing powders that make the laundry even whiter, or the incontinence medicines, without a second thought or unnecessary dilemmas.

"How have you been?" I asked.

"Oh, same old. Buttering up the clients and generally lowering the bar. How about you?"

"My patients keep coming to me with the same problems. So we have similar feelings."

I had to ask her about the land of Black Harpists, but I did not know how to go about it. And if we do not know what to say, let us try to tell the truth.

"Excuse me, Verdana, but you have to help me. How do I get to Skeletons Lake?"

It was then that I realized how much the word "friendship" means. Because Verdana looked deep into my eyes and said concisely:

"Go to hell!"

"But let me explain..."

"I already said everything I had to say," she did not hide her anger.

"Verdana."

"Fuck, do I have to explain it to you in block letters? Forget about this conversation, forget the damn Skeletons Lake and go back home."

Apparently, I put her in an unapproachable mood. I left the Mad Hatter with more questions than answers. Because what exactly pissed my friend off?

***

I think I mentioned that it was only the first of several attempts to get information. My next stop was the British Aggressor pub. A guy named Gollum was waiting for me there. He owed his nickname to a skin disease that caused him to lose all body hair. As far as I know, he did not have any inclination towards jewelry though. He worked in a corporation, I think in property insurance. Above all, he was an incorrigible lover of everything that was associated with horror.

"What did you want to learn from me?" Gollum went straight to the point.

"Remember, we talked about the Harpists once..."

"Sure thing."

It was Gollum who told me a long time ago about the creatures living in the walls and ceilings. You can even say that it was thanks to him that I contacted the inhabitant of my ceiling.

"How to get to Skeletons Lake?" I decided not to waste time.

He looked at me with very serious eyes.

"Do you realize that this can be a one way trip?"

"When I am there, I will find a way to come back," I gave him the only answer I could tell at this point.

"The way is relatively simple. Suspend the rope to the ceiling, climb it and voila! You're there!"

I could not believe that the solution to my problem was so fabulously simple, practically waiting at my fingertips.

"Where is the catch?" I wanted to know.

"The catch? You hammer the hook* to the ceiling, you hang the rope on it and..."

"It can't be that easy," I interrupted. "How do I get into this damn ceiling?"

"This will happen automatically. It would be different if you did not know that the passage to Dreamland was hiding there. Then of course it would be impossible. But you know where you want to get, you realize that this whole story is not a futile figment. The most important thing is to believe."

---

* it is a wordplay, a catch and a hook is the same word in Polish

"I don't need to hit the ceiling three times? Loop around the second star and swirl clockwise until the morning?"

"Oh, you just give the password."

"What password?"

Gollum looked at me slightly dumbfounded.

"Well, I don't know it. It's your dreams not mine."

"Eh. In fact not mine, but Majewski's."

"No, you misunderstood me. The Land of Dreams is common to everyone, but the gates to it are, so to say, personalized."

"But where do I get this password?"

"You can just dream of it. If you fall asleep with this question about the password for about three months, then the dreams will finally reveal it to you."

"Three months? I don't have that much time," I replied.

Gollum frowned.

"In that case, you have to talk to a hacker."

***

It took me a good part of the evening to reach the abovementioned hacker. I had to make a round trip through the nightclubs of the capital. It was not an elementary matter, to find a hacker specialized in dreams. I knew many of these computer specialists from the time when I had an extensive psychiatric practice. This time, however, I needed directions. A journalist dealing with paranormal phenomena gave them to me. And here I was going to meet a guy called Wątłusz*.

At this hour, the city pulsed with a subliminal life, but to the observer's naked eye it could appear deserted. After two in the morning, the urban landscape undergoes fundamental changes - the places of entertainment are just points shining in the dark, scenes taken out of the context of the night. Sometimes, a night bus will

---

* funny nickname derived from the word frail/thin

pass along the street, almost as full as during the rush hour, although the passengers are slightly different from the afternoon ones. Sometimes a taxi turns quietly at the intersection, carrying a couple, busy with erotic rituals, with it.

Wątłusz lived in a new, gated neighborhood, not too far from the old town. He let me in through the intercom and then personally opened the apartment door. If the view of the mustached guy in the evening gown surprised him, he did not let it show.

When we went to his living room, he offered me a drink with an umbrella, then he realized his mistake and prepared two whiskeys with ice. We sat down in deep armchairs, very comfortable, so probably ergonomic.

"How can I help?" He asked.

"Relatively easily. I need the entrance code for Dreamland. I don't know the password for the gate in my ceiling," I know that all this sounded quite absurd.

Wątłusz smiled.

"Of course you realize that it can be dangerous..."

"There is nothing left to discuss. I need to get there."

Wątłusz 's smile has widened even more.

"I don't mean your trip, in fact I don't want to know anything about it anyway. My point is that simply hacking the database can be dangerous to your health. And, I would say, in a tragic, irreversible way."

I did not care. The procedure itself indeed looked unusual. I got some kind of a drug, after which I fell asleep, then Wątłusz connected me to his computer using electrodes. I woke up an hour later with a dressing on my forehead. The dream hacker looked at me, obviously amused.

"So? You have this password?" I could not restrain my curiosity.

"Yes. It reads: 'password123'."

***

I'm in my office. I hammered a suitable hook and carefully tied a rope. I am standing on a stool, whispering under my breath the password to access the gate leading me to another world. It seems to me that I see a face on the ceiling, looking at me expectingly. "Password123" - I repeat a little louder now, and a passage opens in the ceiling. I check again if the loop will withstand, then I tighten it on my neck.

***

Streetlights are beginning to go out at dawn. The bird graffiti artists eagerly start leaving their musical tags on trees growing here and there. In a moment, the sun will rise, unless something unexpected happens - in the end, one can never be sure.

The first or last (depending on the point of view) passersby sneak among the fading shadows. And now we rise slightly higher than the street level, and we reach the height of the second floor. From here we can comfortably look through the windows, of course, provided that we do not mind the blinds, curtains, or shutters. Fortunately, the view of Vinicius Winnicki's cabinet is not blocked by any artificial barriers. The external observer, whom we became for the purpose of this unique scene, turns on the zoom. The window gets bigger, gradually filling the field of view. And we already see everything that we want to see.

The office is tidy. The piles of books, falling over, or the files of handwritten pages, which even yesterday were a dubious decoration of the room, are nowhere to be seen. However, this is not the most significant change. Because yesterday at this time the office was empty, and now someone is staying in it. If you can still use this expression. That someone is Vinicius Winnicki. The psychiatrist's body sways on a rope hanging from the ceiling. A look of surprise is stuck in his face, compounded by the purple tongue protruding from the right side of his mouth.

Chapter 12

MARTHA

I felt like thinking of the past today, and I came back to the time when we were still a completely normal family. Maybe I longed for the peace of mind and the kind of a ritualized bor n that characterized our lives until recently. For example, half a year ago...

It was evening then, the kids were complaining as usual, saying that they did not want to go to bed yet. Marc and I watched a movie, and of course we had to stop the screening every now and then. In the end Kallen almost fell asleep sitting and had to be carried to his room. Sophie probably understood that she would not be able to continue her theater on her own any more and she too went to bed. So we sat with my husband, the movie ended, and we sipped wine without any occasion. I remember a feeling of total fulfillment overwhelming me. Marc also had to feel good because he looked into my eyes and said:
- Sometimes I forget how much we have achieved. Our children, this house, us. You know, it's a bit like sitting in the first class of a plane, and it's been circling over the city for a long time, and then it suddenly descends to land, drops safely on the airport runway. And so on, the pilot thanks you for your trip with them, you can hear the applause from the economy class somewhere behind you - what a shame, and I just went through half of the sky to get to where I am.
"You must not forget about it, ever," I replied.
"About the passengers' applause?" He smiled.
"Stop it, you know what I'm talking about."
"Yes, of course, I know."
We were both silent for a moment. Suddenly Marc's eyes flashed and I knew he would want to tell me something. It is not that we can

get to know anyone completely - yes, sometimes we smile at the same moments, we say identical words at the same time, knowing that only this other person can fully understand us. However, there are secret paths of mind that we always follow alone - unless we invite someone to go on a journey together. This look of my husband was just such an invitation.

* * *

I'm not sure right now if I remember his story well. He recalled his rather early youth in it, which he spent in college in Salzburg. He drank the best coffee of his life at the Alter Market in the city of Mozart, this is also where he met friends with whom he wandered in the shadow of the medieval fortress, when the wind was moving curtains from the old houses that bowed to the tourists. That city is gone, it got lost somewhere among the blue waters of the streams behind the horizon of modern technologies that came after the student period of my Marc's life. In any case, he met a man named Egon there, with whom he attended the same classes for a semester. Egon was a passionate mathematician and once described to Marc an algorithm ideally guessing the reading preferences. I remind you that it was before the era of the Internet, contextual ads and websites that could recommend a favorite book based on your previous likes. Marc's friend's method was based only on mathematical equations. With their help, he was able to calculate whether a book would appeal to a specific person. Interestingly, it was also possible to deduce the earlier book delights from the calculations. My husband mentioned a few funny situations provoked by these exercises. For example, Egon calculated once that a certain girl would be love The Lord of the Rings. It turned out that the girl was allergic to the fantasy in any form and ridiculed the friend's algebraic arguments. Egon, however, could not be discouraged easily, and somehow persuaded the distrustful woman to give it a try. About a month later, the girl started dressing up as an elf and going to all the conventions. A story that was almost cruel in its perceptiveness also happened. One of their snooty friends posed as an extremely well-read intellectual who loved to show off his knowledge of the literary canon among friends. Egon, out of curiosity, checked the algorithm of this alleged intellectual, and it came to light that his favorite book is *500 literary quotes for every occasion*.

I do remember however, that I asked Mark at that time what was the message he wanted to convey to me by bringing these memories. He twisted his face in pretend terror and replied that it was just a story that raised the rather trite topic of the unpredictability of human behavior.

"You know, I never agreed to let Egon calculate my literary favourites... I somehow felt in my guts and not quite consciously, that I would not like the result of these equations," my husband said.

"But see how it could apply," I teased him. "If it can calculate your favorite book, it's good for choosing the ideal life partner as well."

Marc smiled.

"Egon did not calculate my reading preferences, but I in fact asked him for help in looking for love. And that's how we met, honey!"

"Oh, you are horrible!" I shouted.

It was a wonderful evening. I still remember it to this day.

***

Please understand me well - our marriage is really far from ideal. We often argue about some trinkets. In these moments, I'm comforted that we've never argued about really important things. We also often have "quiet days". However, this is not so unambiguous. Personally, I think that anger is a part of the overall peace of mind. We will not achieve harmony without a bit of negative feelings, it is simply not possible to use a simplified scale of sounds. Anyway - it is up to us alone to determine which emotions we will define as negative. Or maybe we should not use such categories at all? Anger does not have to be bad, sadness does not have to tear us apart, regret does not necessarily lead us to be lost in self-accusations. Only the final results count and they are the most important at the end of the day. It does not necessarily mean that every emotion has a reason to exist - sometimes even those that look good at the first glance, lead to negative consequences. I try to look at it this way. Neither me nor Marc are the walking ideals, but there are definitely more good memories than bad ones. Perhaps this buddy of Marc could mathematically obtain the chances of individual people to be happy only on the basis of shared reminiscences? But there was no chance to find it out - Egon's life path had long ago turned in an unknown direction. But now, I in turn remembered something that happened to me, also during my student life...

* * *

I did not spend my university years in an equally picturesque place as Marc. For the sake of explanation - it was not Harvard or any other Cambridge. Alright, disclosure clause. I studied at the Aleksander Gieysztor Academy of Humanities in Pułtusk. Stop laughing. Take a look at university rankings, these ironic smileys will immediately disappear from your face. And if you look for some information about Pułtusk, you will also change your attitude. I do not mean the longest paved town square in Europe, the bishop's castle or the whole range of beautiful, very old churches. This city has a soul in itself, some mysterious union of history and the present, old age and youth, the possible and the impossible. In any case, I studied history then, I read a lot of science fiction and I had outgrown the deathlings for a long time. And yet one day, that childish faith in miracles came back to me.

I used to go to the university on a bicycle. Already then, at the end of the twentieth century, the town was friendly to cyclists. Amazingly, even the drivers seemed to treat cyclists with some respect, which is a rather unusual phenomenon in larger agglomerations.

That day I also rode my two-wheeler. Spring had already settled in Pułtusk for good, the sun reflected in the tiny windows of the houses, the colors were slowly taking on the glow, typical of April and May. I was riding slowly, filling my eyes with the passing views, the atmosphere of a small town slowly awakening to life. At one point, another lover of two wheels rode out of the side street. Dressed in a colorful leotard, he clearly stood out from the Białowiejska Street, bathed in a gray of the dawn. As I stared at the rainbow suit of the man in front of me, I suddenly noticed an inscription on his back. I rode a little closer and then it turned out that the letters formed a rather straightforward message - "follow me!". Puzzled, I decided to find out what this was all about. Probably if I were a bit older, I would listen to the voice of reason, which would order me to go politely to the morning lecture. However, in those days, the kidnappers of young women, who would later end up in German or Swedish brothels, where not in the news as often as they are now.

The colorful cyclist turned several times into more and more narrow streets, finally stopping under an old tree - I guess it was sycamore. I got off my bike, a bit worried, and he turned to me. I saw his face for the first time. He had extremely sharp features - he resembled a bit the New Zealand climber Edmund Hillary. There was some wisdom in his eyes, touched by the blink of sadness, but he smiled with obvious effort. Suddenly, I heard one of the strangest questions in my life.

"Have you ever worn a suspensorium?"

I was speechless.

"What...?"

"Well, suspensorium. Balls protector."

I shook my head in a fake astonishment.

"Why would I do this?"

The guy looked at me with a glint in his eye.

"It was just a test, a control question. In fact I wanted to ask you something completely different."

I slowly realized that the situation was beginning to overwhelm me.

"Well, ask then," I said, because in the end I had to say something.

"Have you ever doubted the existence of all other people besides you?"

I was completely lost in the topic of this conversation. The sun began to flow down to the streets of the city in cascades of rays, the temperature was clearly rising. Meanwhile, I was talking to some mentally ill chap. I thought it probably was not my good day.

"But... I doubted in what sense?"

"In the apostolic sense, on the principle of eating plumage, when you listen to the symphony of the seas."

I had enough.

"Enough of this conversation, dude. I am out of here."

He waved his hands impatiently.

"I know. You have a lecture on historiography, it starts in a quarter of an hour. But do you really want to go to it before you know what I meant with these doubts?"

"I'm not very interested in that. And no, I have never doubted the real existence of other people, it is absurd."

"What if I tell you that each of us has a solid foundation to think so? That each of us really lives in our own personal dimension that no one else has access to? That it is only an emotional act that allows us to move to the parallel reality of another person?"

"Nonsense. Why should it function like this?"

"This is a question for theoretical physicists, or maybe for ethics?" His eagle face contorted in a strange grimace. "I can prove, however, that this is how we operate."

"OK, prove it," I did not want to continue this discussion.

"All right, listen, then. At the moment we are connected by a strong emotional relationship based on anger. In other words, you're really pissed at me, and that makes our dimensions merge for a moment. But in a moment I'll make you stop feeling angry and in effect you will disappear - at least from the slice of reality that I occupy."

Now he at least got me curious. I was not sure what the trick he wanted to do would be, but he certainly intrigued me. Suddenly, however, everything darkened in my eyes and I realized that I was losing any interest in this matter. The branches of the tree leaned over me, and with them, all the light-shadow games in the bends of the bark and the fractal structure of the single twigs, merging into the mighty labyrinths of the branches. I must have lost consciousness for a moment, because suddenly I was shocked to find that I was sitting in the St. Matthew room, and Professor Wybicka was telling something about parenetic literature, or some other subject distant from my thoughts. What actually happened? Did I just fall asleep in class? This would explain the whole thing to some extent, but it did not explain later events at all. For in the following days, I repeatedly had impression of being followed. In addition, I felt, almost all the time, the doubts about the presence of other people in my life, expressed in conversations. It was as if the Rainbow Hillary's theory was becoming a self-fulfilling prophecy, which - as one can easily imagine - was driving me crazy.

And then, after a few weeks, everything calmed down. Gradually I regained my balance, I started to make new acquaintances without major problems - and I did not wonder every time if I was dealing with a living being or just a dummy of someone's presence. I can't say that I completely forgot about this strange event, but it slowly moved to the ethereal, openwork past, hidden behind muslin curtains. Sometimes the memory came back in unexpected moments, like when I was making love to Marc for the first time, but it did not carry with it the tedious belaboring the possibilities; it was like a glimmer of a soul affected by a familiar melody or smell.

***

The next day Marc and Alfred were going to Radom. Will they be able to learn something that will restore the normality? However, remembering those student days, I came to the conclusion that the standard is always some kind of unattainable ideal, that the everyday life also hides secret passages and never opened chambers in itself. How often something happens that snatches us from the usual pattern of thinking and makes us redefine even the most obvious truths... Perhaps this peace of mind to which we aspire, is also just an idea, a non-existent line connecting the sky and the earth somewhere in the distance? I would like to be sure, to have the unwavering faith that our actions, made for the happiness and future comfort, will never lead to any side effects, such as suffering and pain. But peace of mind has many components - as we have seen - and perhaps not only anger is one of them, but also sorrow.

Marc went to bed early, and I stayed in the kitchen for a few moments. I had a lot to think about, and sometimes it's the late hour that is the best moment for such reflections. I boiled some water, poured it over my favorite herbs, I looked out the window for a long time, wondering if the glass sheet protects us from what is hidden deeply somewhere in the mind. Of course it did not protect, because this time the danger did not lurk somewhere behind the fence, but it was quietly waiting for us in our own home. I drank the brewed drink, put the cup in the dishwasher and turned off the kitchen lamp. Then the bathroom, how close and how alien at the same time, and the evening rituals associated with washing off the make-up and other necessary activities.

I went to bed full of anxiety, a tugging and persistent one, which did not have much in common with the fear of falling asleep. This time I was much more afraid of the awakening.

SOMEONE ELSE DREAMS. VI

I've been watching too many drama series lately, I've eaten too many spicy dishes. This may explain my peculiar dreams, which I do not remember in the morning, except some fragments.

My name is Perdykalomenopaulos and I am a muse. Hold on, I can see the image of a winged maiden in a skimpy dress appear in your imagination! You fall into thought stereotypes, but in the end, what can you expect from the children of the Age of Consumption? False sparkles, half-truths worse than blatant lies - this is your everyday life. So I will explain it straight away in simple, stony words - I am a man. Ha! I am an archetype of muscular masculinity with a height of several dozen meters. (I use the lengths of modern times so that you do not have to reach for encyclopedias and calculating machines... appreciate this gesture...) Enough? I know exactly where such absurd ideas come from... The reason for the confusion of concepts are the centuries of indoctrination and propaganda of mediocre third-rate poets... But think logically for a moment: why the hell would a sculptor need a goddess with manicured nails? Will such a minute-posture girl be useful when you have to push a stone block off a cliff, or pull a tree with roots to hold a Chryselephantine sculpture?

Somewhere in the middle of the fifth century before Christ, the enlightened Athenian people voted for an amendment to the Artist's Profession Act, whereby men could also be the muses of sculptors, painters, poets and other freeloaders. This decision did not surprise anyone - you have certainly heard in your times about Greek love... The vast majority of the pantheon of our creators professed the ideal of a feeling with homosexual predilection. Even my master sometimes looked at me with strange eyes, and indecent thoughts were probably rolling in his head. Fortunately, I was several dozen times bigger than him!

I felt most uncomfortable when I posed for him for hours and he carved my likenesses depicting Hellenic athletes. Ah! You can probably find out what I looked like! But it seems that twenty-five centuries later, all that's left from my master's life works are miserable Roman copies, which certainly do not reflect the power of my masculine grace.

So my master sculptor specializes in works showing characters in motion. Sometimes I wonder, what is the sense in binding human bodies in marble. How strange, however, to see these sculptures stopped on the run as if in a movie frame (ha! I did my homework and I know something about your century!). I think I'll never understand the artists, but it's not my worry. I only help them in their search for inspiration. Well - sometimes I also clean and pose...

I remember when one day we went out in the open air to find an idea for another statue. For some time now, the master had been suffering from a creative block - earlier a sculpture of a runner was created, a long jumper (a human figure suspended in the air on invisible threads looked strange) and a javelin thrower. Myron - that's my master's name, and if you have not guessed it on the basis of previous premises, you know shit about classical art - got more and more annoyed. That day we just sat in the olive grove, staring at the sky. And suddenly a strange flying object appeared to our eyes, whose shape resembled a disk. It was coming out of the clouds like an emissary of the gods, but its only divine attribute was the fiery flames emerging from its base. After a short flight, the item landed a few hundred meters away from us, and the smile that I knew very well appeared on Myron's face.

"Perdykalomenopaulos! I will carve a pitcher! Take the disc in your paws and stand with it next to that tree!"

I never tried to argue with him when he had that smile on his face. I ran to the landing site of the mysterious thing, grabbed it in my hand (it was not warm at all) and returned to Myron. He showed me how I should pose, then grabbed the chisel. And then the longest torture of my life began...

You certainly know this statue. Can you imagine the uncomfortable position I had to keep for many long hours? It was terrible, but muses must listen to the voice of inspiration. I thought my hands would fall off my torso... (by the way - have you ever seen Venus from Milo? You must surely think that the sculpture has lost its hands over the centuries as a result of salt water, temperature, or maybe volcanic eruptions... Not at all. The model simply posed a bit too long...).

It was almost dark when Myron let me rest. And I just had enough of this damn disk. Without thinking much, I took on the pitcher's pose again, turned around couple of times properly, and threw it towards the nearby rocks. At the moment of the impact, we both heard a bang, and a puff of smoke rose over the cliff. Myron looked at me.

"You did not have to throw it away... But actually, the sculpture is almost ready."

We returned to the city. The master never learned that after many years he would be known mainly as the one who sculpted the discobolus. He probably would not be happy about it, because he thought that his magnum opus was still ahead of him. We all feed on illusions of some kind.

Centuries have passed and those moments from two and a half thousand years ago are slowly moving to oblivion. During this time I had many masters, I experienced countless adventures, and now I am slowly preparing for a meeting with the gods in Hades. I am reconciled with fate.

Only sometimes, just before falling asleep, a strange reflection comes to me. What if some living creatures lived in that disk? Perhaps their remains are in a deep crater, among silent boulders and broken pieces of metal? But this is a fleeting thought, it quickly melts into non-existence. It's not my worry after all, it's a remorse tormenting some other Perdykalomenopaulos. I'm just a muse. I repeat it like a spell and the sleep comes every evening, caring, soothing and gentle. I am a muse, I am a muse, I am a muse. And nothing more.

Chapter 13

MARC

Radom greeted us with the discreet beauty of the Art Nouveau houses and the haughtiness of the glass skyscrapers in the city center. Okay, I was kidding. Eve ̦ an guess how Radom greeted me[*]. I was here for the first time in my life, and from the very beginning I felt that I would come here again and again. We arrived early in the morning, when the town was still in a sleepy mood, and people wandered aimlessly down the streets, lawns and pavements. Fortunately, I had GPS with me, so finding the address of the secret library did not cause us any problems.

"I did not think it would be the city center..." Alfred pointed out.

"Come on, there is nothing outside of the center," I replied.

We stopped at a non-distinctive building at Niedziałkowskiego Street. The nearby park tempted with shaded benches and a fountain, as if it was trying to tear out some urban space for itself. I decided that after visiting the hidden library, we would go to this oasis of greenery. For now, however, an important task awaited us.

This time the secret reading room was hidden in one of the rooms of a flat that looked like a drunkards den. Apart from the weird looking individual who let us in, the Bacchus suite was empty at this hour. The furnishings brought to mind the previous era, boasting coquettishly with cabinet walls and old chairs with springs. I would like to say that the interiors were cozy and intimate, but I would openly violate these pleasant words.

The way to the library led through a corridor ending with a single door. After opening it, we saw an unusual view. In the middle

---

[*] supposedly the ugliest city in Poland

of the room there was a hatch, and after lifting it, we saw a spiral staircase leading down. A few meters below, the kingdom of books began. The library room was huge. The shelves stood under the walls and in the long rows in the middle. Alfred quickly jumped in to search the catalog. Soon it turned out that Codex Sygmanta de Syntagmum simply stood on a shelf next to other volumes. Carefully, we moved the book to a table lit by a small lamp with a stained glass shade. My friend began to delve into its content, and many years of his experience with antique books allowed me to believe that he would quickly find answers to the questions that bothered us. And that's what indeed happened.

"Listen... That's probably what it's all about," Alfred was excited like a little boy in a toy store.

He began to read to me a story of a monk from the late Middle Ages.

***

This old sage told me about his journey, which he took on the holiday of the Annunciation of the Lord in the days of the good old king. I decided to follow his lead, so I crawled on the straw mattress, closed my eyes and waited for a calm to come over me. Angels sang over my head more and more quietly, because what is falling asleep, if not a cut-off song without words? A sleep like a mountain with deep prospects rises above you like the mercy of our Lord, you just have to find the right way. Although in this case it is probably different - this route has nothing to do with Jesus and his teaching. At least this was what an old man, similar to a green dragonfly, told me in his cottage, smelling of dust. We have to go away, move away, be ready for the most terrible of nightmares, because only then will we get to the other side. I asked him if he meant the hell of some terrifying underworld, or maybe the gates to the house of demons, howling at sunset over deserts and oceans. He, however, smiled at me with the fullness of his wisdom and said that there are no

141

religious connotations in dreams, because they are only a reflection in the mirrors, the reversal of a vision, not of the order of things. And there, in these mirrors there are strange creatures playing harps, and plants that our Earth does not carry, and all of this under a completely different starlight, as if muffled, yet still visible. And you can reach them only in one way - by dreaming a terrifying nightmare, which will compromise our sense of oneness, our self, swaying on the bumpy road to the shadow. We will recognize this dream at once, because it will overwhelm us with its vision, with its black, muslin touch. And there may be a pale girl standing under a tree or turning into a bird in it, a dark kingdom guarded by empty armors, a cold space of revelation, or a distant horizon of events. It may be in it, but it does not really have to be. The path without Our Lord is terrible, but in the end, everyone has their own fears. However, the most important thing is to dream these nightmares at least twice the same night. This trail, however, is my trail, the path under the muffled light of the stars, for I walk down the valley towards the Skeleton Lake and I am more afraid than ever before in my life.

**

Alfred seemed very pleased with what he had discovered, although for me the reading aroused only doubts. First of all, I did not have a clue how to use this text in a practical way. Was I supposed to recreate a medieval straw mattress, to rest on it in the faint hope that it would bring a proper nightmare? And this sage similar to a green dragonfly - what kind of a comparison is that? Meanwhile, Alfred looked at me with sparks in his eyes and said:

"Let's go to this park. I'll explain everything to you there."

And that's what we did. In the park, aptly named "Tree Lodge", we sat on a bench next to a bust of a Chopin, or maybe it was not a bust but a freestyle stone impressionist work, bringing to mind flames around the composer's head. Autumn leaves on the trees added color to this creative craze - more of the sculptor than of the creator of the Polonaise in A flat major. The sounds of the big city did not reach here, and it was as if we found ourselves in a completely different place, a little dark despite the multi-colored frame.

"There were a few key elements in the monk's story," my friend began. "First of all, the effect of a meditation, a specific tuning for the right channel of dreams. You can read about it in the guidebooks for controlled dreaming..."

"And what else?"

"Short repetition time. You must have the same dream twice during the night. This may be the hardest thing to achieve," Alfred worried.

"I don't know. I don't know anything about this stuff. And how to dream a really terrifying nightmare? I had the impression that these appear every night."

My friend looked at me with obvious compassion.

"I'm afraid, Marc, that this truly terrible dream is yet to come."

"You don't know what you're talking about," I protested.

"I know very well. I guess I haven't told you about my childhood nightmare, which really made me panic."

"I don't think so."

"There weren't any monsters in it. There were no terrifying faces in the walls, no shapes growing out of the wardrobes or from under the bed. My terrifying fear was caused by a drawn sea."

"What?"

"You know how children draw sea waves - kind of sinusoidal lines, densely next to each other. In my dream, these lines were waving like on the screen of an old black and white television, but that's not all. These movements were accompanied by a sound somewhat reminiscent of the humming of a transformer, but with a rhythmically changing frequency. Each time this drawn sea appeared, I woke up with a loud scream. And you know what? I do not remember any toothed monsters, werewolves, cannibals or witches, but I remember that nightmare to this day."

"What did it mean? Have you wondered about this?"

My friend's face now looked just like a paper mask set between shadows - pale, without a drop of blood, with a terrifying grimace.

"You know, I think I'll just drown someday."

∗∗

We were returning from Radom with a sense of a job well done. And yet the memory of the conversation at the Tree Lodge park would many times bring frightening associations with that strange expression on Alfred's face. Is it possible to dream of our own death in the same way as to move in a dream to the land of dreams, and wake up in it in a physical reality that does not exist in the ordinary dimension of human perception? A bit like in this famous story, in which a young man visits a paradise in a dream and picks one of the paradise flowers, and then wakes up and sees its stem, and its inflorescence as a colorful stain on the pillow.

I knew that I would have to take on a very difficult challenge. But I had to break this magical circle of madness that drove my whole family crazy. Even before arriving to Warsaw, I realized that I remember all my dreams very well - probably because I tried to write them down. Now I just had to get a book about a lucid dream (Alfred promised that he would bring me some interesting reading on this topic), and then fall asleep, and let myself be invited twice to the most terrible nightmare of my life. Piece of cake.

Chapter 14

SABOL

Holy moly, how happy I am not to be an actor anymore! It's a nice thing, no - a calling, a mission, being a self-existent work of art - everything is right. But I could not ?se interpersonal relations, because you must know that the so-called "circle" is a bundle of snakes and a mainstay of all kinds of vermin. Backstabbing was probably the most popular game in our class, and later, in theaters or in the acting agencies, it only gets worse. And, of course, spending time with people who have the highest opinion about themselves - quite the opposite than about others, drunkenness and drugs, this whole pathetic professional solidarity! Ah, and the directors - like the priesthood caste, narcissism and pretentiousness! A nest of vipers, one worse than the other! Eh, sometimes I regret it, but in comparison with the artistic milieu, here, in the Police, everything looks almost ordinary. Wow, the conclusions I reach after years of work! Way to go! Although today it is very far from normality...

It all began in the morning, with the inspection of the place of the alleged suicide of Winnicki. Well, obviously the word "alleged" is a formality to protect our asses in this case, because the guy hanged himself, no doubt about it. Śmigielski and I arrived at his office a little after ten. A funny story - we got an anonymous phone call that we should have a look at this address. We were supposed to interrogate the guy again, so Śmigielski said let's go. The door to the flat was open, and in the doctor's office there was an additional chandelier made of his body - have I recently mentioned a self-existent work of art? We called for investigators, technicians, a doctor - the most ordinary procedure in the world. While waiting for them, I looked at the bibliophile collection of the deceased.

There was enough stuff to look at, although I rather do not like books. Someone once told me that I look very moronic when I read. I appreciated the opinion of this person once... anyway, never mind... Meanwhile, Śmigielski's face all brightened at the sight, and oh, how the idiot smiled at the shelves. It was very inappropriate behavior in these circumstances, no, but that's how it is with Śmigielski. Long time ago we were going to a New Year's Eve party, except that he had some book to finish and stayed home. I don't understand it, I just don't. And yet the fixation of my friend helped us a lot.

"Oh, Jesus!" He shouted at one point, staring at the bookcase like a puppy at a chew toy.

"What happened?" I asked.

"The guy had a whole collection of books on drugs. A few words about hallucinogens. Cooking methamphetamine in a weekend, LSD for dummies, there is literally everything here!"

"Maybe he used these books professionally?" I suggested.

Śmigielski shook his head and took one volume out of those standing on the top shelf.

"Look! It's a real rarity, totally out of print! Encyclopedia of the drug baron! Just ten copies were issued, each of them is signed with the name of the recipient! Let's look. And what we see? Signed by: Vinicius Winnicki."

I thought about it for a moment.

"Are you saying we should press Bison to spill out everything about the doctor?"

"Who knows, maybe it was him who rocked the whole beat? It may turn out that he was responsible for the transports of this new stuff."

Śmigielski has couple of flaws, and one of them is a certain lack of flexibility in opinions. In other words, if he fixates on something, once he creates a theory in his pretty sharp mind, he is pig-headed about it. I felt that it would be so also in this case.

"Relax, Śmigiel, don't get crazy. Of course, we will interrogate Bison, but something doesn't seem right in this whole story."

Of course, I did not have the slightest chance to know about a certain contradiction then. After all, if Winnicki could move to the happy hunting grounds or anywhere else, by using his drug, he would not try to do it with a help of a rope hanging from the ceiling. But this is just a digression, I would find out all about this much later.

For now, I asked the technicians to investigate the crime scene very thoroughly. Yes, a crime, because if there could be mafia works involved, we could not rule out the serial suicide theory. However, I had to wait for any conclusions until I would see the results of the autopsy.

"Bison will not be too pleased that we are dragging him to the Headquarters again," Śmigielski observed.

"Well, he won't. But maybe he had already arranged something, no, regarding our trip from Warsaw to Hogwart?"

***

The return to our offices took us surprisingly little time. A lot of credit goes to Śmigielski, who talked all the way about a book he had just read. Its protagonist apparently participated in a galactic competition of lifting weights, representing Earth. The intrigue assumed, as my friend explained to me, that sports competition was just a cover for the game of space intelligences. Śmigielski quoted entire passages, from which I only remembered that a green man with the body of an insect and the dragon's head became the galaxy champion.

A lot of work awaited us in the office. It turned out that someone had stolen the precious model of the old Luxtorpeda railcar, known to all as the Flying Hamburger*, from a friend of the chief

147

commander. The top brass went crazy and everyone had to abandon current cases in search of a diesel train in cito mode. Fortunately, the stolen bauble was quickly located - the guy forgot that he had lost his Hamburger playing poker the night before. Around four thirty I made another appointment with Bison. He was supposed to visit us the next day around eleven. Of course, in the company of his silent lawyer.

Geez, sometimes I regret that I did not become a professional actor... Dealing with lawyers is probably even worse than wrangling the fucking movie directors. A dude came once, even more beefy than me, we knew that he for sure damaged one old woman, all for a miserable pension of a few hundred zlotys. He did not want to talk, then his lawyer came, told him to shut up, and what? We had to let him go, and then the granny was accused of an assault, because it seems that she had trashed our hero a bit with an umbrella. Fortunately, she got a probation.

Bison was again smiling like a Colgate commercial guy. It turned out he had good news for us.

- Okay, puppies. I will have the goods for you, but of course we have to sign an appropriate contract. Well, you know, you will not arrest me for possession or anything like that...

"Don't worry, we're recording everything," I said.

"He, he, he... We, too," Bison laughed, casting a meaningful glance at his lawyer.

"When will you provide us with this sample?" I Śmigielski asked.

"Don't you worry, in the evening, somewhere on the borough. Will you let me propose my own location, dogs?"

We looked at each other and nodded.

"Where and when?" I decided to be concise like a motherfucker.

---

* The inhabitant of Hamburg, no similarity in Polish to the food

"In the Alibi pub, today at 10 pm. My man will be sitting at the bar. As soon as he leaves, take his place. The bag will be taped under the seat of the bar stool, there is just enough space there."

"We are glad Bison, that you're cooperating. Especially since we have, no, more questions to you," I brought the stern expression of a tough guy on my face.

"I'm not sure, doggie, if I feel like talking," Bison smiled.

"That's it, fucking trash. Tell me what you know about Winnicki's organization, or I lock you up for forty-eight, and I'll throw your pub guy in the cell in the evening," I yelled.

"Relax, no need to raise your voice." The gangster held up both hands. "My answer is: nothing. I don't know anything about any Winnicki's organization, I have no idea who Winnicki is. I never heard that name."

"Are you sure?" Śmigielski cut in before my angry retort. "We suspect that he was the one behind bringing this new drug shit to Poland."

"Ah, that's why this question! I understand, I understand..." Bison had now a much calmer face than a few moments earlier. "I assure you that no Winnicki brought a batch of hallucinogens to my area. My people did it."

I noticed that the mafia boss's lawyer was not very happy with his client's exuberance.

"I mean, not specifically mine, just some people I know." The thug began to retract.

"And you say you don't know Winnicki?" I asked.

This time Bison was thinking about the answer a bit longer. Finally, he exchanged a look with his lawyer and smiled.

"You'll get this information. Everything we know about a Winnicki guy. Of course, it probably isn't his real name. I will send you an email tomorrow."

"Well, we have an appointment then." Śmigielski said quickly. "I'm especially curious about this email."

Bison shrugged.

"I will do everything I can."

When they left, I looked at the deputy chief.

"Let's do this: we get this stuff in the evening, you go to get it, okay? And tomorrow we will wait for this email and then we set off on a journey, okay?"

"Of course, boss."

SOMEONE' ELSE DREAMS VII

I protest! These nightmares are killing me, I can't take it anymore.
I'm seventy-five and I really deserve a rest

The sun was still hiding behind the mountains when Alex climbed the Lion Rock. The city pulsed with thousands of everyday affairs. Knights sneaked out to mistresses or ran from their enraged husbands, and the children stretched out their hands toward the clouds, looking forward to the Ceremony that would take their childhood away from them. Alex, however, was too high to hear the sad singing of Mothers and the sounds of joyful adultery. He only heard the sound of his blood, flowing through the corridors of his body and falling in waterfalls onto the flat plains of his heart.

He felt the breath of a rock that called him with every stone and all its structures. His life was slowly fading away, he was becoming a part of the Call.

When the sun, driven by the wind from the east, shimmered over the ruffled turrets, he stood at the top. He cast a farewell glance at the City, which gave him his name and took away his hope. After a moment, he spread his wings and flew off towards the mountains.

Carry me, wings, behind the last curtain of sleep.

I want to touch clouds and stars, before I fall into the stony void of awakening.

Ivonne was looking out the window at the sunlit streets of the city.

At this hour they were empty, except for the children playing and the winged shadows of the Guardians who were circling somewhere up high, looking for any signs of disrespect for the law. Her eyes quickly found Vagh, who, together with his peers, took refuge in the shadow of the strelitzia. He was her youngest son and the Ceremony was awaiting him soon. He will surely pass it successfully. She knew it, but somewhere deep in her heart, behind all the curtains of Faith and Tradition, Ivonne was afraid that Vagh could become one of Icaruses. When she thought about this eventuality, her wings *trembled and she fled to the farthest corner of the Nest, to be alone with her fear. The Possible is much scarier than the Inevitable, because it falls on us like a stone. Like an awakening.*

Lion's Rock is on the planet Hermes V circulating in the Bass system. It plays an important role in the beliefs of the natives, for whom it is a place of ritual suicide. Closer details on this subject are unknown and like the entire religion of the Hermesians, they are shrouded in mystery.

The light of the day was slowly disappearing in the crawling twilight, as Aspar, Ivonne's husband, and Vagh's father, returned home. The Ceremony was to take place the next day, and the City was preparing for the holiday. Architects were suspending their columns high among the clouds, painters were finishing covering wings with religious images, and flying dragons were soaring in search of delicacies for the holiday tables. Only those, whom fate ordered to face the ritual the next day, shrouded with the mist of secrets and suppositions, meditated in the silence of the home nests. Aspar found his son staring at the sky, shimmering outside the window.

"Tomorrow you will be a man already..."

"Or Icarus."

Aspar could see his son's grim face, his shrunken figure and wings waving in an uncontrollable impulse.

"That's why I'd like to say goodbye to you. In both of these cases, you will become someone else... Maybe a stranger."

Vagh looked away from the stars twinkling in the sky and looked at his father.

"It's a tradition, right? Fathers always bid farewell to their sons the day before the Ceremony?"

"Just like mothers do with their daughters." Aspar replied.

"Well, the tradition has been done. Can you leave me alone now?"

Aspar left. Later, he lay for a long time next to Ivonne, trying to fall asleep, but the dreams were gliding somewhere behind a stone wall, unable to find any breach in it, through which they could fly.

Once upon a time a little girl ran to her mother, crying, "Mother! Mom! Look! It's snowing outside, although it's the middle of the summer!" Her mother looked out the window and said, "It's not snow, daughter. It is your father who flew from The Lion Rock." Then she called her uncle and together they began to pick the white feathers, and the wind danced furiously between them.

The Master of Ceremonies was looking at the gathered in the Hall. His face was hidden in a wooden cage - a symbol of the function he held, and also the associated prestige. The hall hung many meters above the ground on special columns, whose crowns disappeared high in the clouds. Swallows were flying between them - The Messengers Of The One Who Never Awakes.

"For He gave us wings, thanks to which we can fight the wind and the fate of stones." But He also said "Not all of you will be worthy of clouds. But some will reach even higher." And that's what happened.

At that moment, the rays of the sun burst into the room, bounced off hundreds of mirrors and fell dead to the floor.

"Those who will succeed today, will become the full members of our community. Men and Women. The fate of the Icaruses is awaiting for the rest - they will never know Space or Emptiness. And one day, the One Who Never Awakes will call them in the voice of The Lion Rock to give them one flight, one touch of His hand. Their wings will cease to be dead. Glory be to His Mercy!"

The Master of Ceremonies stopped. In the silence, disturbed only by the murmur of the wings of the Messengers, the first sounds of the bird choir could be heard.

"This day can come in a week, a month or many years. Nobody knows the paths of the Lord! We only know that we are his dream, and He is our dream. Let the ceremony begin!"

The course of The Ceremony is one of the greatest mysteries of the inhabitants of Hermes V. We only know that it is called a Dream in a Dream. The candidates are given a strong soporific drink and fall asleep. After waking up, some of them become "Icaruses". The mechanism of this selection still remains a mystery to our scientists.

Vagh flew over the city. From this height, it resembled a brown corpse decaying on green grass. Every few heartbeats it disappeared behind the clouds, to appear a moment later even smaller and even more dead. He felt the vibrations of the air, caused by the movement of the monstrous wings of the One Who Never Awakes. He knew he was flying before His face. This was the very essence of the Ceremony - meeting face to face with God. A kind of the Last Judgment, because in a sense, there were only two possibilities: Salvation or Condemnation. Suddenly there was a flash and a huge cliff appeared before Vagh's eyes, with a bottomless pit boiling at its base. He saw the other participants of the Ceremony, who must have gotten here before him. A few of them were falling. They became Icaruses, a certain variety of stones. There was awakening awaiting them down there. What was waiting for him? Suddenly he found himself over the cliff. He saw God.

The revelation took the form of a huge horse with wings reaching the stars. The One Who Never Awakes shone with the glow of the sky reflecting in his marble body.

Dream in the Dream, God in God, Man in Man. I will rise above the City and feed the wings with Your Glory! And if that is Your Will, I will swallow the Space in one gulp and fall to Your Feet! Life is a Dream and an Awakening, a Flight and Falling, Music and Death!

"Welcome home, Vagh." Aspar could not hide his emotions.

The nest was decorated with thousands of dead and living birds. There were pigeons and hummingbirds, parrots and phoenixes, peacocks and cormorants. Ivonne ran to her son and embraced him with her wings.

"I was so scared, honey."

Vagh looked at his parents. At their faces, marked with a grid of wrinkles, at their falling out feathers and their love, which they cultivated for so many years of their lives.

"You must have known everything..."

"What are you talking about?" They were surprised, their naive tenderness he know so well showing in their eyes.

"In the end, The Lion Rock calls everyone. Not only Icaruses. We are the land of suicides."

"Nothing lasts forever, son. Praise be to Him Who Never Awakes!"

"And if He ever wakes up, then what? Will we disappear like characters from a dream? Or maybe we will slowly blur until He forgets about us, just as we forget the birds we dream about?"

"Remember that He is our dream too."

"So what is real then?"

"Only the stones and the wind."

Release me from the cage! Let me get besotted with Emptiness for the last time! Let me out of the prison of the gravity! But before you start Dreaming, check if you closed your eyes...

Chapter 15

MARTHA

Marc did not come back until late in the evening, when the city slowly settled down to sleep. The moment I saw him, I already knew that the trip to Radom was a suc   , by the evening glass of chardonnay (children, of course, had long been in beds), he told me what he and Alfred had discovered. My husband emanated joy, although the past weeks certainly left a mark on him. And not only on him. I was terrified by our children's hallucinations, I was fed up with the nightly horrors and the whole atmosphere of madness around our lives.

As for the bizarre hallucinations, well... I also lived my own hell. For several days, it seemed to me that someone made a subtle change in my person. I did not recognize myself in the mirror, I noticed with horror that I was using a slightly different mimicry, as if I were expressing emotions, experiences and moods unknown to me before. I started gesturing during the conversation, which never happened to me before. These gestures became untranslatable emblems, their meaning was unknown to me. Who lived in my body, who nestled in my mind? As if I was torn out of the whole context.

But now, a chance to end this nightmare appeared.

"So you have to move from your worst nightmare right to the land of dreams, right?"

Marc nodded.

"I am not entirely sure how to do it yet. Together with Alfred, we will wade through the literature on the subject. I must learn to control my own dreams in order to dream of this magical portal."

I thought about it for a moment.

"Oh, dear, so... You know... Isn't there some contradiction here? Because, look, you want to consciously create in your own mind a transition to a dreamland. But at the same time, you must have a terrible nightmare, and this twice during the same night. Can you really control this? Who deliberately closes his eyes and orders himself to do something like that?"

"I don't know, honey. It all sounds like a madman raving, but we can't live like this anymore."

"You're absolutely right," I agreed.

But I was already thinking about something completely different. Why did I smile when he started talking about a nightmare he was forced to immerse himself in? Where did this strange gesture I made admitting him right come from? There was an alien being in me, I stopped controlling my own body and emotions.

We went to bed quite late, and I closed my eyes very reluctantly.

***

I dreamed that my head hurt. It was not an ordinary pain, like a dull pounding in the skull, but a real migraine, pulsating, recurrent, merciless. In a dream I woke up from time to time and then these untrue awakenings relieved my suffering, but each time I fell asleep again and the pain came back. The most terrible thing about it was the cruel inevitability of the recurring attacks, and the awareness that I can do nothing to break out of this loop. At one point it even seemed to me that I noticed decorative gates framed with ivy. It was probably a consequence of my evening conversation with my husband. I must have been influenced by him.

At any rate, when I woke up in the morning, I was terribly tired. And - surprise - I started to have a headache.

***

Marc left the house early.

"I'm going to Alfred," he said quickly and touched me with his good-bye lips. The children were at school. I sat down at the kitchen table to prepare my daily schedule. Shopping, reheating dinner, picking up children, writing an overdue article to "The Most Beautiful Lady of the House" - it was quite a lot. I wondered about the next point when the phone rang.

"Hello?"

"Is this Mrs. Martha Majewska?"

"That's right, but... Who's speaking?"

The voice in the receiver dripped with cordiality and sweetness.

"Do you feel uncomfortable lately, as if someone moved into your mind and introduced his own order there? Are you alienated?"

"Yes, but who is it?"

"We invite you to a meeting at the Joyful restaurant at Snow White Street on Friday at 4pm. We will present the latest auto-massage device, and you can also win a very attractive prize."

"Bloody touts," I thought.

"I'm sorry. I'm not interested," I interrupted the sweet monologue.

"But you can come with your husband. There will be a raffle and..."

"Thank you, goodbye," I hung up.

By the way, they almost got me this time. Why did they try to tempt me with such arguments? It was as if they knew that...

What the hell! I decided that on Friday I would go to the Joyful restaurant. Curiosity, the serial killer of cats, got the better of me again.

***

The average age at the show of the latest Simassaggio Merdacinese* device of the third generation oscillated around

---

* means "Chinese shit" in Italian

seventy. At the very beginning, a young boy in a suit encouraged everyone to participate in the raffle. The condition was to complete a survey with a lot of personal data, so I skipped it. The show itself resembled the performances of circus magicians and I must admit that the dashing youth was great at it. Some people took out their IDs after just a few of the smooth sentences spoken by him. It works the same way every time - smoke and mirrors, a calm and familiar tone of voice that is supposed to make every listener feel special. And of course the uniqueness of the situation itself - the device would normally cost about eleven thousand zlotys, but on that day it could be bought for just four thousand nine hundred and ninety-nine zlotys and ninety-nine cents...

"Can you imagine how useful the equipment like Simassaggio Merdacinese is? Please tell me how important health is for you? Your health and that of your relatives? - encouraged the young man in a suit. I knew all these tricks perfectly well, I even wrote an article about the sale of pots once. So I decided to pretend an interest and talk directly to the salesman. I had to ask for this statement from the telephone conversation that someone had moved into my mind. I knew from experience that after the main show, there would be time for individual conversations with potential buyers of the miracle device. And indeed, that's what happened."

I talked to another young wolf in a suit. At the beginning he asked my name.

"Mrs. Martha, you are one of our youngest guests here. How old are you, twenty-five?" He answered when I introduced myself.

"Oh, no, I've been over thirty for a long time," I said.

"I simply do not believe you," he objected. "And I will not believe until I see your ID card. Do you have your ID?"

I decided to play according to his script for another moment.

"Here, my document," I said, handing him a plastic ID.

He looked at it, and I noticed a wonderfully faked shock in his eyes. And then he said something I expected.

"Tell me, shall we write a contract for the data from this ID?"

"No, we won't. Better tell me, how did you know that I have problems with alienation recently?"

The man looked at me sharply.

"Well, let's put aside those learned sales talk. I know exactly why you came here..."

"Really?"

"Really. You came here because of the Harpists."

This time, I was genuinely surprised.

"What do you know about Harpists?" I asked.

"Will you sign a contract?"

I laughed. A seller through and through.

"I will think about it."

The guy smiled.

"The case is quite obvious. The Black Harpist who protected your family against bad dreams was killed. It was probably done by White Harpists. It was, however, only their first move. Now they will want to drive you crazy. You must stop them."

"Do you know how to do it?"

"I would not be here if I didn't know. The problem is, I don't want to tell you that at all."

I was surprised again.

"How come?"

His eyes glittered.

"I am here to sell you Simassaggio Merdacinese, ma'am. I can't do anything else yet."

"You can't or you don't want to? You are a bit inconsistent in your story."

"You can consider it the trick of an experienced salesman."

The situation was at least stalemate. I guess I had to put everything on one card. In the end, the peace of my children was worth much more than five thousand zlotys without a penny.

"I will buy this equipment of yours. And you will tell me what to do with the Harpists."

"Well, we have a deal then," he replied. "We will now write a contract, and then we will arrange a conversation in a quieter place. Someone might overhear us here."

I sighed and fulfilled his request.

* * *

The salesman who, as it turned out, had a proud name Janush**, was supposed to come to us on Sunday. Over another night drink - this whole situation will lead us to alcoholism - Marc and I talked about our further plans. Apparently, many Buddhist texts from hundreds of years ago talk about the control of dreams.

"You know, it turns out that our idea for writing the dreams down was a shot at the core of the target. According to textbooks, this is the first step on the way to lucid dreaming!" Said my husband with evident excitement.

"What are the next steps?"

Marc told me that there are several methods to obtain satisfactory results. Supposedly, the easiest way was to set the alarm clock for 2 -3am to wake up a bit. The next dream after falling asleep was supposed to be a conscious dream.

"So we are home," I was happy. "You dream the worst nightmare of your life, wake up in the morning and convince yourself that you must dream it again."

"I know, it will not be easy," Marc admitted.

"It will be unfeasible, in my opinion," I clearly cooled his enthusiasm.

---

* the name became a synonym of a redneck in Poland

"No, it won't be that bad. Apparently just reading about lucid dreams alone helps in achieving sleep awareness."

"What else should I do? Don't tell me that reading alone is enough," I got interested.

"So-called testing of reality is an important technique. It is about capturing some inconsistencies. Apparently you can develop a habit of looking at your hands. Alfred found interesting information in one of the textbooks that whenever we look at our own hands in a dream, they always look a bit strange. They may have distorted proportions, they may be covered with spots, and sometimes even tattoos appear. It is precisely with this that we recognize we are not in the real world, but we sleep peacefully in bed, and everything that surrounds us is woven from the fabric of a dream."

"So from today on we look at our hands?" I laughed.

Except that I was not too happy at all. And I have to admit something. I put up a brave face, but when I'm home alone, I let myself panic. I yell into the mirror, pull my hair out and cry. Thanks to this, I'm still holding up somehow.

Chapter 16

BISON

So far everything played out well, like some heavenly spheres or other "Bachomozarts". I ordered a sample of the stuff to be delivered to the Alibi pub, and then I started to che. ngs. Where have I heard about this Winnicki before? The case had to be under development, except I lacked basic elements. Well, but a man in my business does not have to have the perfect memory for names and faces. After all, they are consiglieri. I called for Aurochs and Daniel, wondering who would reach my hideout first this time. Of course, as I might have suspected, they almost collided in the door.

"Winicjusz Winnicki, I want to know everything about this guy," I started without ado. "Contacts, address, shoe number, cock length, anything you can find."

Aurochs was already firing up his databases, and Daniel grabbed the phone. I poured whisky into the cup - let's give them a few minutes before I get pissed off. Whiskey does not taste good in thick china, but I'm too old to fight bad habits. Sometimes you just have to let go, even in my position.

Ten minutes later Daniel spoke.

"First of all, don't worry, the dude croaked. I have access to the autopsy results..."

"Ooooh, give it to me!" I encouraged him, without even trying to hide my curiosity.

The youngster looked at what he had on the screen.

"Here it is, boss. Only those goddamned forensics use this language, eh. The immediate cause of Winnicki's death was strangulation, i.e. suppression of gas exchange in the lungs."

"He hanged himself, I understand," I interrupted.

"Yes, but here is something more interesting... Apparently, medicine does not exclude that another cause of death could be a cardiac arrest as a result of the reflex irritation of vagus nerve receptors in the carotid sinus."

"Daniel, I don't give shit about that," I interrupted the biomedical show off of my subordinate again. "The important thing is he hung. Do they write anything else? Third party accessory? The chemical composition of the blood?"

"No body marks suggesting possible defense. And the toxicological exams have not been carried out yet. No blood alcohol was found for sure in the body, and other than that we don't know anything."

- So we have a suicide, probably a mentally ill man. How can he be linked to our business?

At this point, Aurochs began to report, which I expected from him. In the end, he earned quite good money, and in addition he was my godson.

"Well, the guy was Veal's and Gandalf's doctor a few years ago. He could also have shares in Colargol's company."

It was old news, last year's snow, and fables for robots*. Even if Winnicki maintained some relations with the underworld, it was once upon a time. Colargol himself disappeared somewhere in the early nineties of the previous century - apparently he left for the antipodes to breed rams or other alpacas.

"You don't have anything fresher?" I asked, but Aurochs shook his head. I thought deeply and refilled the mug with whiskey. There was no thread that cops could use to string us along. In fact, I felt great. In the evening I will send a mail to Sabol, and earlier Daniel will deliver the package to the Alibi bar. Of course, I was tempted to give the police the goods prepared suitably, but I decided that there

* Fables for Robots, a Sci-Fi book by S. Lem

is no point in creating more enemies than necessary. Let's call this law Bison's razor, he, he.

So I gave the appropriate orders, and after a while I was alone in front of my laptop. Now only this e-mail to Commissioner Sabol. But of course, the moment I got to work, I felt that someone was staying in the room besides me. What the hell? I looked around carefully, but I did not notice anyone's presence, and yet... Someone's eyes pierced my back, somebody's light breathing caused air currents, and the silence around me swelled with anticipation. At this moment I understood that the wall was looking at me. I noticed with amazement delicate changes in its texture, which gradually began to resemble a face of a bizarre being. I was overcome with terrifying fear, I felt my heart being flooded by hormonal cascades. Oh, why aren't my soldiers by my side? I tried to make a loud shout, but in a chilling fraction of a second I realized that I would not be able to do it. My mind began to roam the distant trajectories - it fell somewhere in the gutters of the rainy suburb of Montreal, suddenly appearing on a lazy market in an Italian town, sailing across the oceans of air over the fastidious streets of Switzerland, then falling with a terrified cry to my feet; I was standing paralyzed in a sudden disturbance of the balance between the need for the oxygen and its supply, as if I were drowning with somebody's knees pushing me under the surface of reality.

Suddenly I fall, or maybe it is only the floor approaching my face, the Persian carpet invites to the land of a thousand and one nights, for a short moment I even forget that I was supposed to write this damn email.

***

Aurochs feels like the king of the world. Professionally, he has never achieved such a fulfillment as he did today. He even thinks at the moment that everything worked out well - he did not go to work for a bloody corporation after graduation, instead he gained experience in the family business. He abandoned his academic career, he would probably have a postdoctoral degree now instead of the latest BMW model. He gets into his car, starts it, and then enjoys the sound of the improved V8 engine for a moment. Or maybe he should go somewhere outside the city, lower the side windows and feel the salty wind in his hair, as he used to when he cruised around in the old Polonez? It's some idea to diversify this great day. But no, he can't, he must come home early today, he promised his daughter that he would help her practice dance steps. With some regret, he abandons the idea of a night drive and goes to the main access street leading to the neighborhood where he lives. He still thinks of the old times expeditions along the forest paths, when the huge truck Renault Magnum pushes him into the carrying elements of the new flyover.

***

Daniel goes to the Alibi pub, looks around carefully, pretending to be slightly blinded by the light of the street lamp, and then goes to the shady side of the street. He, in contrast, feels extremely lousy today. Probably a cold or other bug, in any case, the images blur to pixels, the head is pulsing like the announcement of a strong hangover, and the muscles are shaken by uncontrollable tremors. He will take the parcel to the place, and then a quick transfer home, bed, warm tea, vodka. Longer sickness is out of question, it would be a violation of a professionalism, because he would have to stop training then. And Daniel is going to run in a marathon in May.

Except he will never finish any longer run, he still does not know that the bird flu virus got him, and in a week he will spit his lungs out in the intensive care unit. He will be one of the first victims of an epidemic, and if anyone thinks it's a nasty end, it could always be worse. Daniel will miss the zombie apocalypse, another pension reform, and the lost world hockey championships.

SOMEONE ELSE DREAMS VIII

My dreams are completely indistinguishable from life. Equally irrelevant, full of prosaic events interspersed with a mystery that I am not even aware of. But maybe this is what they should be like?

As soon as my sons hurried to class, I went to the laundry room. I put the laundry in, this time dark clothes, then I took dry clothes out from the dryer and returned to the apartment. One pile is my underwear, the second one - my husband's, the third Witold's, and the fourth - Andrzej's. The piles grew on the couch like prehistoric woods - blouses, pants, and sports clothes. Items needing ironing in a separate stack. Then I just need to carry everything to the rooms, and now I can devote myself to musings. For better thinking, I wash dishes after yesterday's supper and after breakfast at the same time. Suddenly, I remember that Witold was supposed to take the test on some prayer in a religion class and he most probably did not pass. My blood pressure jumps up, I fall over and lose consciousness. But not completely.

Suddenly I soar somewhere under the kitchen ceiling, noticing my body creating a bizarre figure. The passage of time loses countability, gains other structures. The boys enter the kitchen. Witold screams in fear, and his older brother tries to calm him down.

I open my eyes, I must have dozed off on the kitchen chair. Right, of course, I forgot about the pan and the pot. I approach the sink, I pour dishwashing liquid. I wonder what I will watch on TV tonight. All these new movies are so brutal, and the actors have speech impediments, and even if you can understand them, you hear only vulgarity. Such are the times. I stare at the stream of water flowing from the tap. My eyes are getting heavier with each passing moment, more and more tired, as if pulled down by a weight, hung on the eyelids. I get into a trance, I am relaxed and my soul is flying under the ceiling again.

The boys are trying to wake me up. No luck, I'm completely unconscious. "Why don't you call an ambulance?" I think, but I do not know how to make them hear me. Or maybe I do? Andrzej takes his cell phone and yells something into the receiver. After a while, I am happy to see that he is trying to do CPR. I open my eyes, but I do not see my son's face.

I fell asleep in my chair again. I'm still dizzy, I feel an impending migraine, but maybe I will manage to make the dinner before it comes. All the ingredients are ready. I put the water on for pasta. The apartment is once again an oasis of silence, a sanctuary of repetitive activities and gestures. I turn on the radio. The DJ makes a contest for listeners, I give it one ear, while stirring in the pot. Polyphonic jingles somehow rhyme in the air with the sound of a spoon hitting the metal. At one point, the radio presenter tells me to close my eyes. And again, in my sleep, I fall asleep.

The boys are bravely waiting for help. They seem so small from above, although they will soon be teenagers. My body is lying as if lifeless, even though it is brimming with emotions. Suddenly, I hear loud banging on the door, and a moment later two men appear in the kitchen. I feel a peculiar anxiety and fear at their sight. Maybe because they don't look like paramedics at all? They are both wearing black coats that seem to heave like on a helicopter landing pad when the machine slowly approaches the ground. In addition, I have the strange impression that they know very well about my soul, powerlessly suspended above their heads. "Leave me alone!" - shout the thoughts, unable to get out, trapped in the transparent cage of my head. One of the newcomers lifts the inert body and throws it on his back. At this moment, the second one approaches Witold and Andrzej, pats their heads and says: "Go back to bed, boys. Your mother was ill, but now everything will be fine." They both leave, closing the door behind them, and I can't leave this apartment, can't follow them. Oh, I have to wake up now, open my eyes, go back to the preparation of this damn dinner. But how to do it when I'm no longer on the cold floor, next to the boys, trembling with fear? I know that they will not see me again, that they will testify in a few hours, but none of them will be able to describe any of the mysterious men. Andrzej will say that he has never seen them before. Witold will not say a single word for many weeks. I will be gone without a trace, and the Police will not be able to explain who the kidnappers were.

And yet I wake up. I have less and less time, my husband will soon be back from work. We'll sit down to dinner together, he'll tell me that this fucking Jonathan took it out on everyone again, that the quiet streets of Philadelphia are not so calm at all when they fill up with a million cars returning home, that he has a headache again. I will try to steer the conversation toward the topic of children. The biological clock is rushing forward mercilessly, it is time to start trying to grow the family. But he will shut me with some fancied argument, because we can't afford, because there is recession, because our lives will change irreversibly. I will just nod my head and clean the dishes.

Chapter 17

ŚMIGIELSKI

The Alibi Pub was located in Warsaw's Anin, at Bronisław Czech Street. Inside, it was rather empty, although there was a match on the TV hanging behind the bar. I sat in the   , took out a book from my backpack - I was reading John Brunner's novel 'Everyone in Zanzibar' - and discreetly watched the situation. There was an old man in worn jeans sitting on the bar chair - was that what Bison's man was supposed to look like? After a moment, however, a bearded guy in the type of an eternal student approached him.

"Get out, grandpa, this is my place!"

The man looked around the empty pub with a slight surprise in his eyes. However, he had to see an irresistible encouragement in the bearded guy's eyes, because he got up quickly and moved by the window with his pitcher. The student sprawled comfortably by the bar and ordered a drink. It seemed that I could read for a moment.

"I saw doodles on the house wall doo-doo-doodles on the wall-all house hou hou house all wall what I saw I forgot so it could not be anything important A KIT FOR POLIFORMING WILL LET YOU FEEL ON YOUR OWN HANDS WHAT MICHELANGELO AND MOORE RODIN AND ROUAULT FELT we will analyze your metabolism and prepare a special mix designed only for you after which your trip will be higher longer faster a cross between a kaleidoscope and a computer allowed us to create a collisionscope in which your dismal everyday environment becomes a wonderful mystery."

Enough, the guy is getting up.

***

I walked quickly to the bar and took the place left by the student. I regretted that I was on duty and had to limit myself to non-alcoholic Lech. For a moment I discussed with the bartender - a graying hippie whose ancestor was probably a Chinese - the aftermath of the centuries of invasions that our homeland experienced. The guy knew all about dystopian fantasy.

I was watching a bit our football players, who were just fighting in another match of last chance. At the same time, I tried to blindly scrutinize the package hiding place in a restrained way. After a while, I felt a packet attached to the bottom of my seat. I detached it with unnoticeable gesture and quickly put it in my pocket. Pretending to finish the beer calmly, I touched it again and again, and then left. Patience has never been one of my strengths. In the car, I gently removed the top layer of foil and it turned out that there was a small bottle inside. It contained a few bright yellow pills that seemed to vibrate very lightly - although the latter could have been attributed to fatigue, because it could not be the effect of the non-alcoholic beer. For a moment I felt quite a strong temptation to swallow one of the tablets without Sabol's knowledge, and for an even shorter moment I hesitated whether to empty the whole portion down my throat. Depression is a strange condition, I'm telling you. Doctors still argue whether it is a disease or a disorder. Looking at the clinical picture itself, several dozen types of this condition can be distinguished. Long story anyway. I was lucky that even though I had suicidal thoughts, I never made any attempt to take my life. The funniest thing is to follow my reasoning - I just thought that my death would not really care anyone, would be a completely insignificant episode and therefore suicide makes no sense. This is twisted, I know perfectly well. In any case, I refrained also this time. The next morning I was to go on a completely different trip.

* * *

Sabol stared at the neon yellow dragees with obvious bewilderment. I also had to admit that it was hard to see formidable drugs that could change the very fabric of reality in these candy-like shapes.

"Okay, youngster, as they say - mosquitoes are foraging, let's get inside."

I looked at Sabol and then I understood. Today, he took on the role of the sinister Doctor Plama.

"OK, OK, easy, commissioner. Have you checked your email?"

Apparently he did not - this was the answer I read from his rather lost look.

"Ah, right, right... Email from Bison, it can be important, no? Stop looking at me like that. Excuse me, prince, this boy has a hangover."

For the time being I had enough of Hydro-puzzle*. The more so that, as I suspected, the drama would take place in the setting of the raging elements.

But Sabol's mailbox was empty, of course not counting spam, which the IT policemen still fought unsuccessfully. So it looked like we had to make an important decision on the immediate future.

"I want to ask you something, Commissioner. If we go in this shit together, will you stop this jugglery with movie quotes? We must approach the matter in full concentration, you know."

Sabol looked at me and nodded quickly.

"I regret that I will not quote today the statement that the language of gold is the only Esperanto, but that's fine."

"You don't know how happy I am about it, boss. Well, I guess we are calling the HR to request a personal leave?"

Fifteen minutes later, we left the hospitable walls of the police station. We were going to my place - this choice was to provide us

---

* Polish superhero parody movie from 1971

with a bit more privacy. The weather outside was perfect to try to move to a different climate zone. It was raining, raining again.

I thought that if a yellow, burning ball that is our nearest star appears in the sky one day, many people will report the appearance of an unidentified flying object.

* * *

In the end, the well got me. Every time it seems impossible to fall into the same trap, and yet. And yet, fuck. The strength to fight ends slowly, and then it is tempting to lose myself in the landscape, walking straight ahead while I still see something. To melt abruptly in the blue of the sky, fall as a shadow on the illuminated grass, or less pompously, flush the water in the toilet behind myself. Or just the opposite - to not go out of the well, just dissolve in the groundwater. What's worse, that's what people want, and I see only enemies everywhere. I would like it to be a part of my novel, but it's worse than that, because it's the life. And unlike the book, it will have an ending that I can't have any influence on. Okay, enough of this self-pity, there is a case to be solved, and Sabol counts on me.

* * *

It was a complete absurd - to get stoned on some suspicious stuff, in order to magically move to another world, inhabited by creatures who play harps and send people dreams. I even thought how the media would deal with us after everything would already come to light, if it would, which we could not rule out. Even worse, it was quite likely that our colleagues would find our dead bodies, and then there would be lots of gossip - about alleged mental illnesses, junkies in uniforms, or about homosexual lovers who set out on their last trip together. I wondered if there were similar dilemmas going through Sabol's head now.

"Do we have to, no, suck on it, bite, swallow or sniff?" He asked.

Apparently I overestimated his empathic abilities.

"I don't know the answer, commissioner. Let's try to swallow it."

"You think it will not be harmful?"

"Unfortunately we have no such guarantee."

"It's a bit sick, isn't it, Śmigiel?"

After all, he carried some human impulses in himself.

"I can take it first," I suggested.

"Under no circumstances. What if we then don't find each other in this wonderland, no? We have to do it simultaneously."

I agreed with him and took a Coke zero out of the fridge.

"So, count to three?"

***

At first nothing unusual happened. And then everything began to wave like at a sick party, among the stroboscopes and jigs, by the deafening thud of music, in short - we lost the clarity of vision. Then stars appeared above our heads, but they looked quite peculiar - like silvery toys suspended on strings and yanked by an invisible hand. It was like a puppet show, but it was a fairy tale you would not like to show to any child. A distant atonal music also started to reach us, we could not recognize the instruments, or maybe these were distorted voices of people? My room has long ceased to look like a place where I've lived for a few years; as if something turned it inside out and now the outside and the interior exchanged their position. And indeed - the ceiling gained the clarity of the night sky, the walls gave way to rocky columns and trees, and the carpet was overgrown with grass. Everything fell silent all of sudden. Only our restless breaths disturbed the unearthly peace of this place.

Sabol got up and looked around carefully.

"Fuck, Śmigiel! We made it!"

"Couldn't have put it better myself, officer," I replied. Although I would probably refrain from vulgarity, I thought.

None of us asked the question that was obvious at the moment - what are we going to do now? For now, we were looking around our surroundings, and the view was really amazing. After all, everybody can have a break for commercials sometimes.

Chapter 18

MARC

I look at my hands carefully, but they look quite ordinary.

Holy shit, I did not fall asleep at all! I am beginning to fear that before I learn to control my dreams, they will start to control me. A book reading the reader, or something like   And I thought that I had just the worst nightmare of my life. This time I dreamed that I woke up in the middle of the night. Magic realism - escalated to verismo, because I heard the ticking of clocks, a scratching somewhere in the attic, and other ordinary noises. A luminous corridor opened in the wall, which I followed. It ended with a closed door with a fairly high clearance above the threshold, so I could see that someone was behind it. I also heard a voice that spoke to me in an unknown language. At last I reached the end of the corridor and pressed the doorknob. In the dark room there was a naked woman standing with her back toward me. "Pretty shapely" - I thought and then she began to turn in my direction like a figurine of a dancer. She looked almost normal, but her face had wrong proportions - it had a wide forehead, and narrowed toward the bottom, resembling a cone. Suddenly the woman smiled at me, and I saw several rows of sharp teeth. I woke up. Then I fell asleep again, and when I looked at my hands, they looked quite ordinary.

Strongly shaken, I was preparing breakfast for myself. Martha came and hung around the kitchen for a moment. This afternoon the salesman out of this world was supposed to visit us. We were very curious about what he had to say to us. Martha pointed out that we really needed further instructions. "Let's assume that by some miracle we will get to this land in the wall. Even if so, we don't really know what we actually have to do there" - she said.

The guy promised to come for a coffee after dinner, while in the evening we would be expecting Alfred, who had been persistently searching for information about the Harpists world for the past few days. Yesterday he called me, clearly excited, but he did not want to reveal anything over the phone.

I'm still thinking about one thing - what weapon will we be equipped with there, on the other side? Will there be any fight in the common sense of the term, or will the possible clash take place in a different way? Who will actually be there against us? The Black Harpists were the good ones, and the Whites belonged to the opposing team. But did it mean that we had to defeat the whole gang of these Bad ones? I had certain hopes that the day would shed light on all of these issues.

And for now, I was eating scrambled eggs with mushrooms and listening with growing interest to the kids' conversation. At first I thought it was about a computer game or a fairy tale they had just seen. Suddenly, however, I understood that they were talking about me and Martha.

"They are going through these corridors, and from the white walls emerge... something like ghosts. If you had the right weapon, you could shoot at them. But you don't have anything," said Kallen.

"And what was next?" Sophie was curious.

"We stopped because a bad white man would not let us pass. You know, Daddy said then that if you want to be embraced, open your arms."

"And what did the white man answer?"

"I don't remember exactly, something that love shines in a dumb heart or something like that," said Kallen.

"And then daddy... took out a sword or a wand, right?"

Kallen shrugged.

"Sophie, it was not like that at all."

"How was it then?"

"Daddy knew he had to use right words, like penguin Kowalski. And that's what he did."

I listened to my children like enchanted. Maybe Kallen told his sister his dream, which could turn out to be a prophetic dream? Maybe the power is in the quotes, provided we use them in the best possible way? Or maybe I am raving in the morning due to lack of sleep, and the chronic lack of normal dreams?

"What are you talking about?" I asked Kallen.

"I was dreaming about a computer game, Dad. We were all in it, but as small LEGO figures. It was a bit strange, I must admit. Although not as strange as Sophie's dream."

"What did she dream about?"

"She was sitting at the desk and filling some tables or crosswords on the computer. Whole day, non-stop. And at the end of the work, the devil came and said she has now been spared three nights of hell."

I was beginning to be afraid of my own children.

**

Finally, it was time for Sunday coffee in the garden. This time in the company of a certain Janush, the salesman who pressed my wife to buy a massage device. I must admit that the name did not match the appearance of our guest - I would associate him with the names like Arkadiusz or Mieczysław, if you know what I mean. Young, confident, well dressed, or - as people say these days - "dolled up". He did not bring to mind the guardian of secret knowledge at all, but in the present world it would be futile to look for people, whose appearance reflects the actual state. Some mendacious time we live in, I will tell you that.

We sat under a spreading umbrella, which protected us from everything except the sun. Fortunately, the day was not too hot. Although summer did not give up yet, the fall was now handing out all the cards.

"I will tell you in a moment what the thing is." Janush quickly tuned into familiar tones. "But I must first make sure that the equipment has arrived safely."

Martha nodded. Simassaggio Merdacinese was delivered yesterday by a courier company. Apparently, the massage was even quite pleasant - I decided to take my wife's word for that.

"Well, let's get to the point then. By the way, excellent coffee. What kind is it?"

"Dallmayr Classic," I said. "Can we start?"

"That's exactly what I intend to do. The most important thing you need to know about the White Harpists - they never take prisoners, and fight as if they were immortal. Well, maybe because they are immortal," he laughed.

"So they can't be defeated?" I wanted to be sure.

"It's two completely different things," the salesman said. "You can remove them and neutralize them."

"Oh dear, I mean... What do we have to do?" Martha wanted to know.

"It's easy. They must achieve a whiter shade of white."

"Like in Procol Harum, right?" I was irritated.

"Not exactly. I would like to draw your attention to the fact that in the original song, it is a whiter shade of pale," Janush clarified.

"Stop word playing with us," I said. "What the fuck do we have to do? Use washing powder?"

"You just have to outtalk them. You need a Bard."

This time Martha had enough.

"Where the hell are we supposed to get him?"

"I'm telling you right now, Martha. From your own feelings, from the memories, from quotes. The fourth verse of the mentioned song says that if music is the food of love, then laughter is its queen."

"Can you be more specific?"

"Of course I can, Martha - like every salesman, he knew that frequent repetition of the name of the interlocutor increases the power of the message. - Talking to the White Harpist will be like a game of riddles. The one who will answer the questions correctly, who will use the appropriate paraphrase, an ideally matched quote and so on, will win the battle."

I thought back to the children's conversation this morning. Somehow, it confirmed everything that Janush was talking about.

"All right, Mr. Janush. Tell us how to outtalk them."

"Marc, please let's get on first-name basis. Have you ever heard of quotology?"

"Is there such a thing?"

"Yes, of course. In colloquial language, it's how we call the speech of a person who abuses quotes. Recently, however, there is a separate area of knowledge that uses the quote as a carrier of information - sometimes highlighting, and sometimes negating the original meaning."

"Could you make it clearer? Since he wanted to be with me for you, I stopped embarrassing myself. "

"I will even use the support of scientific papers, if you want. According to Luis Van Der Vette, we use quotes in extreme situations, when our own words are unable to bear the burden of thought. And yet there is a strange transmutation then - because we have to translate our reasoning into the language of another person. It turns out that this transformation is accompanied by the emission of magnetic waves of a rather virulent character. And now you only need to use another quote to direct the beam of these waves in the right direction, for example to our opponent."

"How was this discovered?" I wanted to know.

"Probably in the same way as most other discoveries, by accident. Perhaps some academics were throwing quotes from scholarly works back and forth and at some point one of them lost consciousness? Maybe there were many such cases and someone finally put two and two together?"

"OK, let's assume that all this is true. We just need to have that Bard. Where the hell can we get him?" The moment I asked this question, I already knew the answer. So did Martha, because she exclaimed loudly:

"Alfred!"

Janush was looking at us with satisfaction, as if he had sold ten auto-massage junks in one instant.

***

And late in the evening, we got a visit from Bard, who did not even know he was a Bard yet. Alfred looked like a marathon runner a few minutes after crossing the finish line. I had no idea that the research had absorbed him so much.

"Guys! I know what you have to do!" He started at the door.

"What WE have to do, my dear," I corrected him.

"How come?" He did not even try to hide his surprise.

Martha hugged him in greeting.

"We also learned a thing or two..." she explained.

We sat down to vodka, and then a six-pack of beer arrived on the table. Oh, wait! I'm sorry - it was twenty years earlier. This time we sipped whiskey.

It turned out that Alfred found a study of an old myth about the Harpists. They were immortal beings, but they were subject to all sorts of metamorphoses. One of such transformations was an apparent death, after which they moved to a different level of existence. As a result, they ceased to visit people's dreams and began to control the dreams of other Harpists.

"Whiter shade of white..." Martha whispered.

"Walls in the wall," I added.

Alfred had no idea what we were talking about. I began to clumsily explain my idea - that the land inside the wall must also have some buildings, and without a doubt, these are built of walls. Perhaps the place of the final condemnation of the Harpists was a multidimensional wall in the wall in the wall, and so ad finitum... I noticed that our friend understands less and less of what I am talking about. There was no way out - we told him everything we had learned from Janush.

"Hmm. And how did you get the idea that I was supposed to be a Bard?" It was not difficult to guess that this would be his first reaction.

"Elementary, dear Watson. I laughed. "I don't know anyone else who has read as many books as you."

Alfred smiled.

"And how do we actually know that it's about the quotes from books? The term "bard" implies rather an expert on song lyrics. Or maybe it's about movies?"

"Drop that false modesty, my dear - Martha said. - You once said, I remember it well, that books are the source of all art and pop culture, that everything comes from them."

"Yes, we argued about it then," Alfred nodded with a smile.

"There is no better candidate," I ruled.

There was just a small technical issue left to solve. Assuming that I am supposed to dream the worst nightmare of my life in order to reach the magical portal, in what magic way would I get Alfred and Martha into my dream? I was not alone in these doubts.

"How can we dream a dream together?" Martha asked suddenly.

This issue required reflection, no doubts about it. Meanwhile, however, Alfred unexpectedly had already began to study it.

"Relax, I read about a similar phenomenon many years ago. It turns out that shared dreams are very common, only we usually do not realize it."

-"What do you mean?" I asked.

"A simple example: you are dreaming of a familiar person. There is a very high probability that at the same time this person is dreaming of you. This is not always the case, but scientists today can induce this phenomenon. And I know how to do it."

And then Alfred talked about the experiments carried out by American researchers dealing with somnology. The issue of common dreaming arose completely accidentally in the research on some sleep disorders. Generally, it can be said that dreams come from a very primitive part of the brain, located in its back regions. During the sleep, large fragments of the cerebral cortex are switched off, while the amygdala, responsible for fear and emotions, is strongly activated. The researchers concluded that if several people are similarly stimulated just before falling asleep, there is a good chance that they will be connected by a shared dream. Of course, the study of this type of phenomena only became possible when the brain scanning reached the current level of technical sophistication.

"In a dozen or so years, it will be possible to process scans of a dreaming brain and display them as images on the computer. We'll be able to watch our dreams," Alfred said dreamily.

"Cool vision," I interrupted. "But what impulses are used to stimulate the brain before falling asleep?"

"They must be quite diverse. The script I read mentioned listening to the same music, repeating the same spell, or strong traumatic stimuli."

"What do you suggest?"

"I suggest... Nirvana. The name suggests an increased ease in achieving the desired condition. Let's choose the favorite disc. Maybe Unplugged in New York?"

Martha was not a big fan of Kurt Cobain's band, but she nodded.

"We also need to visualize the three of us before falling asleep," she said.

"In addition, we can repeat our names quietly," I added.

"It sounds quite reasonable. And how will we stimulate the centers of fear?"

Alfred shrugged.

"All three of us will dream the worst nightmare of our lives. I think that this way the amygdala will be perfectly prepared," he replied.

So we had a plan. A controlled dream, or actually three controlled dreams, which are to be frightening like never before. Then, awakening at three in the morning and convincing ourselves that we are to return to the same terrible world again. Of course, full synchronization. It should result in a joint physical transfer of all three of us to the gate of the portal. And then all we need is to outtalk the White Harpists, and we have the thing done. Eh, even just the description of it sounded like an exceptionally convoluted madness.

SOMEONE ELSE DREAMS IX

How I love these dreams about knights! I must have been one of them once, and the subconscious sends me memories like a lost heritage.

"Sisters, we're starting the ceremony..."

The cold moonlight fell on the courtyard and a group of hooded figures gathered in its center. Hooting of owls spread among the cloisters, waiting for a response, but the stone gargoyles were silent.

"Today, we welcome the new members of our Rite - the voice of one of the habit-dressed characters soared high above the ground, scaring the lonely owl."

"According to the eternal ritual, you now have to answer three questions." The voice continued, unaware of the impression it made on the owl. "First of all: who is your idol?"

"Divine Moon, Mother." The choir of the candidates answered shyly.

"Secondly, what is our Order?"

"We're Moon Dust Nuns."

"And finally the third, most important question: what is the main goal of our Order?"

"Rescuing the knights in oppression."

The abbess looked around, but the lonely owl was already on the way to its harbor on an oak branch.

* * *

Indeed, I tell you, our town looks completely new. Yellow-black orioles, still dripping with paint, proudly sit in the crowns of trees along the streets. Green grass, like in the past, on the day of Dawn, encourages the passing merchants to wipe their dusty shoes. A discreet aroma of turpentine floats above everything. The tournament begins tomorrow.

Only two contenders will be in this year's fight. Only they got adequate support in the pre-runs. The scribe Jonah from a nearby castle thinks that, like in previous years, the duel will end in a draw.

Edgar, the Gray Tail Cavalier, is clad in armor that blends perfectly with the color of his purple face. There is a helmet, crowned with the emblem of the brotherhood, on his head. When the knight is walking, his footwear makes strange noises, reminiscent of horse neigh. But this is not Edgar's only extravagance... However, to learn about the other attributes of the knight, you have to follow him to the alcove - this is, in fact, not a good idea.

The other contender is a barbarian from the northern frontiers. His name is hidden behind a shroud of mystery - the provincial office in his hometown burned down during the riots many years ago. Let us call him Zdzisław for ease of reference.

Both warriors are to encounter on the beaten ground. Not very sophisticated way to spend the Sunday, but the middle age have their rights.

* * *

185

Edgar turned only to see the hooded figure that had just called him by name. The mysterious figure knew his true name, which only his parents knew about. Edgar could not allow it. With a snap, he drew a sword from the case on his back.

"I am here to help you," shouted the person in the hood.

"How do you know my name? Answer me now!"

"The more important thing is that you have to fight for the prize tomorrow," said the camouflaged voice, which undoubtedly belonged to a young woman.

"So what?"

"I offer you help. My job is to serve the knights in oppression. Your life is in danger..."

"And you know the spell that will save me from it..."

"I have something better. It's a policy."

"What is it?"

"If you die, your relatives will get a compensation."

Edgar stared at the darkness hidden under the hood. The darkness stared at Edgar.

"Did you say you want to offer it to me?"

The woman in the habit hesitated.

"It's just... a stylistic figure... You have to pay a contribution to the account of the Moon Dust Order."

"How much should I transfer to your account?"

"Twelve obols. But your family will receive the equivalent of ten thousand after your possible death..."

Edgar raised his eyebrows, and his blue face wrinkled like a crumpled banknote.

- "Fine."

***

Zdzisław stared at the fire. A mental effort was visible on his face - or perhaps it was just a trick of light. Suddenly, he jumped to the sound of footsteps. A hooded figure approached the fire.

"I have a policy for you..."

"Huuuh?"

"It is a great spell..."

"Huuuh?"

The individual, hidden from human eyes, shrugged.

"There... Sign here."

* * *

Twang! Kaboom! Twang! Twang!

Both opponents entangled in a mortal grip. The audience watched their actions with bated breath. As the dust settled, two bodies appeared to the eyes of the audience. None of them moved. There was silence, in which one could only hear the hasty steps of the medics, running towards the knights. After a while, everything became painfully clear - the duel, like so many before, ended in a draw. Scribe Jonach mused at his acumen. "Life sometimes resembles a screenplay of a bad movie" - he thought, and a moment later he realized the nonsense of these considerations. "What does a screenplay mean?" He wondered, and the birds were drawing the zigzags of hints in the sky.

* * *

The representatives of the Edgar's and Zdzisław's families banged on the gate of the monastery. From behind the walls came the shout of the doorman.

"Go away please, my good men."

A burly young man waved his ax angrily.

"We came for our compensation!"

"Give us our money back!" People at the gate remonstrated.

"I repeat, go away. The abbess decided that the compensation should not be made."

A murmur of voices rose to the upper registers, and then broke over the walls of the monastery.

"We have the policies, according to which your order owes us twenty thousand obols," shouted the impetuous young man.

"The abbess decided that the insured broke the rules of the contract. They were dueling..."

The group in front of the monastery gate was reeling.

"They were both knights! And you are supposed to get the knights out of trouble!" Yelled the lady in a polyester fur coat.

"General conditions of the insurance prohibit knights from dueling, fighting with dragons and windmills, as well as endangering their lives in other ways," the implacable voice of the doorman continued.

However, those gathered in front of the monastery did not listen to these arguments. It was only after a few hours later, when the city guards shot at them with arrows from rubber bows, that they went home.

***

Two novices were praying in silence in front of the altar of the Divine Moon. The shreds of conversation sneaked into the monotony of prayer.

"I'm not sure if I understand all this. We are to save the knights in oppression. This is what they repeat to us from the beginning. Meanwhile..."

"But we tried everything in our power. It is not our fault that people are what they are."

"Meaning?"

"Unreparable. We gave them a chance they did not take advantage of."

"But we did not lift a finger to help them..."

"It's just a matter of interpretation. Signing a policy, after all, aims to make them think about their own behavior. You can't give men a simple answer like on a gold tray."

"Still, I'm not sure if..."

"Not everything can be dealt with using a spell. Remember, you are a signpost, not a road."

"But the Order gets money in such a dishonest way..."

"Honesty is also a matter of interpretation."

The lights of the stars were slowly fading over the monastery. The owl came back from the hunt, and the remnants of the dinner remained on its beak. Smoke floated in the air, forming big question marks. The owl, however, had already learned all the answers, and now it was just coming back home.

Chapter 19

ŚMIGIELSKI

I was on the other side of the mirror, I broke through a thin crack in the reality, I fled the rope loop that was chasing me. Sabol looked around carefully. The landscape resembled the good Earth, but everything was a bit less intense here - colors a bit faded, angles a little smoothed, like in an old photograph. And this strange light - like in the paintings of the Dutch masters - as it is before a storm or before dusk. I just hoped that the gang of drug traffickers we were pursuing would show up quite quickly.

"It's a dream, no? They can't do anything to us here?" The commissioner wanted to make sure.

"I am afraid this assumption is overly optimistic," I replied. "After all, we are in somewhat physical form here."

However, something else disturbed me. We were alone. Shouldn't someone be waiting here for us?

At least it was clear which way we should follow. We set off on a clearly trodden path that led us towards a nearby grove. With some regret, but also with a visible relief, I found that it was made up of completely ordinary oaks and birches. We moved, trying to be silent. You never know what lies among trees. And indeed, totally unaware, we walked into the first trap.

We were surrounded by a dozen men dressed in white, whose faces were hidden under masks of the same color. It must have been the White Harpists, though I did not see them carrying any musical instruments with them. The tallest of them approached us and asked a very strange question.

"Do thee know the discourse ritual, is not it, or is it so?"

I looked at Sabol and Sabol looked at me.

"We have to ask for an explanation..," I turned to the newcomer.

190

"Dreams are woven from pictures, and pictures - from words. In this world too, words carry the power of the weapon, which sends ghosts towards the greater White. The one whose phrases will turn out stronger, goes on and the defeated one loses his color, moving towards the older dimensions."

"What a babble," I thought, and judging by Sabol's expression, he had a very similar feeling. Well, but gibberish aside, we had to try to face the challenge. The White Harpist looked at us - at least I suppose it was so, and he recited with a lofty voice:

"Scars can come in handy. I myself have one over my left knee, it is an excellent map of the London subway."

This quote reminded me of something, but unfortunately I could not pin it precisely. Then Sabol smiled and replied:

"So if you go in to visit the dungeon

And to steal gold, you'll turn to dust.

Thief, beware, you heard the bell,

Which heralds you a sure, quick death."

And he whispered to me:

"The first part of Harry Potter, I went through it last year."

The guy dressed in white probably knew it too.

"I reflect not your face, but your heart's desire," he shouted.

Sabol responded quickly:

"One can never have too many socks."

It must have been an extremely strong blow, because the White Harpist seemed to collapse inwards. After a moment, however, he managed to croak:

"Truth is a wonderful and terrible thing, so you have to handle it carefully."

However, these were his last words. When he was melting in the air, the same happened to his companions. Sabol turned to me.

"I was good, right?"

I nodded.

"But how did you know which quotes to choose?"

"I had no idea, but I guess the acting experience kicked in."

It was probably a good answer. I realized that we can freely use in subsequent skirmishes the fragments of theatrical plays, and film dialogues we remembered. And after all, I read one or two things in my life. Perhaps it will not be as difficult as I expected.

"Tell me, Śmigiel, why didn't we take out our guns, no?"

"Maybe we'll be better actors here than policemen?" I answered.

* * *

It turned out, however, that police training is also useful sometimes. Over the next few days, there were cases when we had to choose a brute force solution. We were outtalked once, but then it came to light that the White Harpists knew perfectly well what the firearms were for. They couldn't get away fast enough. Another time, the circle of figures around us did not want to dissipate after their leader went down, overthrown by one of my paraphrases. A few shots into the air cleared the atmosphere and our room for maneuver.

We were gradually moving inland. We had the impression that the opponents were getting stronger, but we were doing great. We dropped the napalm of the words of great poets and novelists upon the enemies, threw the exploding charges of comedy dialogues at them, and fired the cocktails from Mrożek and Ionesco. The Harpists could be very well read, but they could not retort well. The years of stage work were paying off.

I don't remember now, which one of us came up with this idea first and shared it with the other one. But I know well that it occurred to us in almost the same moment. In any case, we were sitting by a charming mountain pond (we learned much later that it was called the Skeleton Lake), resting after a battle, and distant harps sang their song somewhere high, amid the peaks.

"We could be the fucking tsars of this place," one of us said.

And then a lot of time passed.

Chapter 20

ALFRED

You never know what gems you can find on the penultimate page of a terrible book - this is my motto. In a few cases it worked perfectly well, I have to admit, as in one bad fantasy novel, in which I discovered a sentence changing my life. Yes, I am a librarian, and reading books has been my passion since childhood. The only thing I regret is its inevitable extinction, partly on the professional ground. After many hours of thinking about books, looking for resources to buy them, discussing the latest bestsellers, and so on, so after all this, layer by layer, you can say that an evening with a book is the last thing you want. I used to read more for pleasure, nowadays I prefer professional reading. That's the fate. But that's not what I want to talk about, after all, I started about something else - about those gems hidden in a seemingly unattractive neighborhood.

Fate loves to play similar tricks with us - all this time you rely on shreds of information, on foggy clues, and then suddenly a secret drawer opens, and you find in it the exact map of the ghost town you are trying to penetrate. You are looking for a stranger from the past, when unexpectedly, an old man in the parking lot hands you his current photo. Things like that happen all the time.

"You have to read this book," a colleague from the Balkan literature department was leaning on my desk. "I bet you'll like it."

He gave me a small volume. There was a name of the writer - Panajot Vithkuqi - on the cover. I have never encountered his work before - I must admit that I have some geographical shortcomings.

"It's kind of Albanian Andrzej Sapkowski," my colleague explained. "I want you to read it because of the really interesting creation of the presented world."

The English title, printed in a rather interesting font, reminiscent of Celtic motifs, was *The Bed Who Sleeps*. I decided to look through the book just before going home. I ended up staying in the library until ten o'clock in the evening.

A writer unknown to me, who was from Albania and whose works had never been printed in Poland, described with great detail the world inhabited by... White and Black Harpists.

***

Vithkuqi did not allow too many shades of gray. In his book, everything was white - like the White Harpists' robes and masks, like their rituals and the sand sifting down the dunes, or black - such as the Black Harpists' costumes, like shadows lying on peach orchards, and the wings of birds falling from the sky. These contrasts, however, did not constitute opposing camps, but rather co-existed. It was indeed true that the Whites sent nightmares on people. But it was interesting what the Albanian wrote about the Black Harpists. They were not at all unambiguously positive figures, after all, these were demons living in the walls of people's houses. Interestingly, in the fantastic prose of the Albanian, they did not resemble the Neanderthals, although their faces were straight from the most terrible imaginations. They were called variously - Black Harpists or Devourers of Dreams. This latter term described our guys quite accurately. Oftentimes people wake up in the morning and can't remember their dreams, they think they did not dream at all. But in fact it is really different - it's the Black Harpists who come out of the wall and devour their nightmares. Because, according to the Albanian writer, there are beings from nocturnal lethargy that could drive everyone crazy. They are White Harpists, whose faces are hidden under beautiful masks, but they are revealed in the darkest hour of the night. Both dichromatic tribes live in small groups, often inhabiting the same areas. Of course - there are no walls on their side of the world - the Harpists enter our homes through the membranes of large, transparent bubbles, floating in the air. The writer solved the question of duels in interesting way - in this world, battles were fought not with swords, but with words. The greatest warriors were those who best mastered the art of eristics.

The goals of both tribes were in fact contradictory, but both sides were bound by the so-called Harp Treaty, signed centuries ago. Under this agreement, no physical contact between the Whites and Blacks was allowed. This implied total immunity and an absolute ban on killing the opponents. Obviously, it was possible to send the defeated in the duel to one of the Inner Dimensions, but in such cases, the Harpist was still able to penetrate several layers into our reality, to harass people with dreams or to devour those dreams.

Under the Treaty, the harpists also devoted to making music together - regardless of their clan affiliation, the Harpists played their instruments almost continuously. They were often accompanied by Singers - the greatest masters of the use of verbal forms of communication. It was them who sang the spells bonding the songs with their magic voices, usually following the vibrating strings of the harps with a certain sluggishness.

The Bed Who Sleeps told the bizarre story of this world, stretched to several thousand years, with time here maintaining its relative property, because the hours passed at a completely different pace than on Earth. For is it not so - here I hung my head for a moment in a sudden surge of reverie - that there can exist empires of almost immortal beings in the universe, whose whole life is enclosed within one blink of a human eye?

***

We set the time for our trip with the Majewskis to start on the last weekend of October - we decided that on the night between Saturday and Sunday we will put on Nirvana's Unplugged in New York, that we will chant the spells of our own names while falling asleep with headphones on. We also decided that a few days before the planned date of transfer, I will move to their house to sleep in the living room. Although the lack of distance in the real world should not be an obstacle, it was better not to risk the completely unnecessary complications. Of course, I gave them Panayot Vithkuqi's book to read, so that they would know what to expect after arrival.

I did not guess that my few days-long visit with my friends would be such a strong experience. I felt as if I got in a haunted house (which was somewhat true); it was not only about the atmosphere itself, but also about the nightmares, which I naturally started to have regularly, but also about some strange vibrations, driving me into a state close to panic during the day. What did I dream of? Every time I moved into the book I was just reading, and these dreamed worlds always constituted a chilling deformation of the reading. It also happened that I played the role of the negative figure in the book, which brought all the consequences with it, including tragic endings. Of course, in such dreams I took over the character's way of thinking with everything it brought along. Pretty funny from the point of view of the reader, but not necessarily from the perspective of the participant.

Finally, the last Saturday of October arrived. The Majewski children were safe with their grandmother, and we were still sitting with evening tea. Everything was ready - Nirvana before falling asleep, acquired skills to control dreams, alarms set for three-thirty. What a nightmare I had that night! I was the victims of the famous film killers in it - Freddie Kruger, Letherface, Hannibal Lecter. Of course, I was fully aware of my role, I awaited the touch of death with horror in my heart, and it was like this every time.

The alarm clock put me on my feet at half past four in the morning, and I kept telling myself that I had to let myself be killed again by a serial killer from the horror. And the dream came back, exactly as I wanted.

And then, quite unexpectedly, I found myself on the edge of a forest. I realized that it was no longer a dream, that no movie archetype was hunting me. However, something went wrong. I was alone.

SOMEONE ELSE DREAMS X

I hate my boss. How many more times will she pick on me for no reason? I can't distance myself and I keep celebrating my disappointments. I'm in a hurry, and hurry humiliates. That's why I have to do something, I have to figure something out at last...

One must make ends meet somehow on this lousy coast smoothed by the lunar, ghostly glow. I used to be a lighthouse keeper, but ever since the introduction of automation, I have been out of work. Eh, I loved those night shifts when I woke up every two hours for a night watch, but that's in the past now. Today, light signals are controlled by soulless electronic sensors that can even activate fog horns if necessary. Romanticism dies, I tell you.

Winters are the worst. In this part of the island, ice rarely freezes the breakwaters, although I remember such years too. If it's snowing, it can even be quite warm. The worst are rainy winters, when a fierce wind from the Atlantic carries with it a sound of sleighs bells and a persistent chill that penetrates the bones. There are days when you can't get out of the house, because the gusts from the sea freeze the blood in your veins, taking away the will to live. In winter, I always get hungry.

What to do in the long evenings, tugged by memories and richly watered with apple wine? You can go to a ghost town near my cottage, wander around the deserted streets, go to a long unused playground. You can then see distant campfires here and there, it's better not to get too close - in these times everyone shoots without warning. Anyway, I do not like people. I am not fond of the empty town, either, I prefer the beach.

The sand sprinkled by snow, small stones measuring the distance from the waves with their rosaries, emptiness. I feel best in this emptiness. I set my imagination in motion, let the riddles from past days resound, the imagination wanders unhindered on the deserted coast. Most often I go all the way to my favorite place on the cliff.

***

I kill the boredom, swallow the nonsense of my existence with the gulps of air, until an idea comes to mind. It may work, it's quite likely. Can you be a lighthouse keeper without your own lighthouse? Well, it's not just a job, it's a vocation. A vocation and hunger.

I wonder what's going on with my wife. Although she died many years ago, there must be someone better informed than me. I just need to find that person, ask the right set of questions, and then I'll know everything. But I do not like people.

Fortunately, I know what to do - my project seems more and more attractive to me. At home I'm gathering all the materials, and then I go back on the cliff.

I light a false lamp to deceive the captains of ships sailing to distant ports. In the persistent wailing of the waves, in the misty glow hovering over the bay after dark, it resembles the light of a nearby lighthouse on Lundy Island. A lie must be similar to the truth, it should even contain a piece of it. And there is truth in it that strikes the plating of the bow with a rocky crest, sending sailors to the last tunnel in which they will see their own illumination. This is one of the most pleasant moments in my foggy life.

***

At dawn, I go down to the beach again. The wind plays its somber melodies in discarded shells, where the very end of the sea begins. A night's tragedy took place a few hundred meters from the shore. The *sea is full of hungry waves, but sometimes it shares its meal with us. So it was also this time. I am slowly but systematically collecting the goods scattered on the shore - perhaps there will be something useful for long, winter nights. But the most important item on the agenda is yet to come. I put all the dead bodies of those who have gone to the last watch in a picturesque pile. I look at it for a moment, and then I go at them. I bite into the cold meat, tear with my teeth, carefully separate what is edible from the bones and other useless fragments. I said I do not like people, but I like them a bit. As long as they are raw. And in winter I always get hungry.*

Chapter 21

MARC

You live with a sense of security thanks to the clear reference systems, in which you place yourself. And then something pulls you out of the frame, sets a completely diff   ghting, makes you look for completely new definitions and concepts. A few months ago, I would not believe that I would try to move into a fantastic world while listening to Nirvana. Kurt is singing, and I try to mentally prepare for the mission we were supposed to complete. Oh no, not me, we never lose control. Now you are standing face to face with the man who sold the world... We can hear the guitar, maybe we should rather look for some kind of harp recording? Vollenweider, Loreena McKennitt? Streetlights are slowly going out at the intersections of the brain. I fall asleep.

* * *

I dream in a completely controlled way, flowers bloom at one snap of my fingers, strangers come up to me on the street and bow to me, animals humbly repeat my name in human voices. I know that I have to complete a task - it's a simple, rather physical skills exercise; I have to walk through a labyrinth drawn with chalk on the sidewalk. I am not afraid of failure, conscious dreaming gives me the confidence I always lacked, but still. I step with my foot on the chalk line, so I have to go back to the beginning. And suddenly, the doubt begins to creep into the illusion of control, I understand that it will not be that easy. And I fail again, I realize in a split second that I am powerless, that all my efforts are doomed to failure. And the worst of all is that I know that no change in behavior will affect the final result, and it will come back like a curse many times over this long night.

This is what this whole dream is about - composed of bricks of powerlessness and several tasks repeating one after another, and while dreaming lucidly, I want to change something in it every time, and every time it gets nastier and fear overwhelms me more and more. Jesus, how I am afraid of this determinism, because I know that in a moment I will dream this again, and I still won't be able to do anything.

***

I wake up to the sound of the alarm clock. What a nightmare it was! I have never been so scared. I know that I will fall asleep again and I will have the same dream. There is no other way to the land of Harpists, I repeat to myself, turning off the lights.

***

I dream again in a completely controlled way, flowers bloom at one snap of my fingers, I light up and turn off the stars the with a movement of my eyeballs, I pull the moon by the neck. Everything is illumination, I live on the edge. Here is a simple task to do - just to go through the labyrinth drawn on the sidewalk with a chalk. I am not afraid of the chalky Minotaurs, I am in complete control of the situation, I finally have the confidence that I have always lacked. Suddenly, what is happening? My foot steps on the chalk line and I have to go back to the beginning. And then doubt begins to creep into the illusion of control, I understand that it will not be that easy. And again I fail, I realize in a split second that I am powerless, that all my efforts are doomed to failure. The fact that I dream in a conscious way, makes my mood even worse - because I am even more aware of my own powerlessness. And suddenly I find myself on the edge of a forest, it seems the twilight is approaching, it sneaks up to me like a cat, oh, I see Martha! But where is Alfred?

***

Martha and I were standing in the peach-colored shadows, cast by the leaves. We told each other our dreams - since Alfred was not here yet, we had to wait for him. My wife moved to her parents' house in her dream. One of the walls in the living room is filled with family photographs - we are immortalized in them, our grandparents, uncles and all sorts of cousins. Some of the photos are large, some are small, some are in color, but the older, black and white ones prevail. Anyway, in a dream, Martha was in the living room, and her mother was making coffee. Then they both sat with their cups at the table and began to talk about various unimportant things - just like it happens in a normal life. At one point Martha looked at the wall with photos and found that all the prints were hanging upside down. She jumped, spilling coffee on the floor, and looked at her mother, who was sitting on the sofa under all these photographs and laughing. There was contempt and malice in that laughter. My wife could not stand it and ran out of the living room. As it often happens in dreams, she moved straight away to our home. Lights were on in the hallway and music could be heard. She switched off the lamp and the music immediately fell silent. Then she looked into the room of our children, who were sleeping peacefully in their beds.

On her way out, she noticed the light in the bathroom, too. She looked in there and found that the tub was full of water and foam. She quickly pushed the foam aside and saw Kallen drowned underneath, who had been lying in his bed just a moment ago.

"It was something unimaginable," she said with a tremor in her voice. "I was afraid most that the dream must return in the morning, if we were to succeed in what we intended. I felt that I would not be able to stand it, I was afraid that in the second dream I would find Sophie in the bathtub..."

"I hope it wasn't like that?"

"No, it wasn't. In the dream replay I only ran out of the mother's living room, and then I found myself here."

"Here" turned out to be a rather specific place. The trees had slightly more intense colors than on Earth, but at the same time, the contours seemed to be slightly blurred. The light fell at a slightly different angle than we were used to. Here and there, huge soap bubbles floated in the wind - much bigger than those that the street animators make in order to delight kids in the squares of big cities.

"I wonder where Alfred is?" I said.

"Do you think his transfer failed?"

"I don't know."

And at that moment we heard him. He was walking toward us from the forest, supporting himself on a carved stick, and his clothes showed signs of considerable wear. I was surprised to find that his face did not look too fresh either.

"Finally you've arrived!" He shouted. "I've been waiting for you forever."

Martha and I looked at each other.

"How come? How long have you been here?"

"A few days, I guess. Unfortunately, in this land there is no division into day and night, so it is quite difficult to assess."

"But... why? How could this happen?" I could not understand.

"Apparently, the time is running here at a slightly faster pace than in the real world. I must have fallen asleep a few minutes before you."

This explanation made sense, and at the same time, it gave me unspeakable fear. It was not a vacation, we have not traveled abroad, rather we found ourselves in a completely alien environment, maybe more unfriendly than another planet. Martha probably thought about the same thing.

"We can't separate anymore. Is it clear where we are going?"

I shrugged.

"We need to locate the Skeleton Lake. A large Harpists camp is located on its banks."

In the book of Panayot Vithkuqi, the inhabitants of this world were nomads, and the only center of power was the gigantic cluster of tents set up in that place. The representatives of both colors lived there periodically, mingling with each other during concerts, jointly managing the whole area of the camp. It had to be somewhere nearby, and anyway - according to the Albanian writer - the whole land was not too vast.

"Let's head towards those mountains," I pointed to the elevation visible on the horizon. "If I remember correctly, the Skeleton Lake is a mountain pond."

That's what we did.

∗∗∗

Along the way, we had a few opportunities to try our bard skills. We fought two or three skirmishes with small groups of White Harpists. Alfred coped with them without any major problems. The first time he used quotes from Ludwig Wittgenstein, then it was John Banville's turn, and at the end, with some hesitation, but also with apparent amusement, my friend used Paulo Coelho's words to live by.

We did not feel hungry, wandering in the Land of Dreams, but every now and again we made rest stops, necessary for the comfort. During them we talked about what was around us, or what would await us when we wake up. At one of the travel breaks we had a guest. It was one of the Black Harpists.

"My name is Kanizet," he introduced himself at the beginning.

He had a really terrifying face, on the one hand bringing to mind the monsters from Hollywood production, and on the other - evoking some atavistic fears. However, you forgot it immediately, when you caught his gaze. And then the tone of his voice - gentle, full of understanding, reaching the registers of radio DJs.

"I know what brought you here. It's about the death of Onizoit. He was my friend."

It turned out that Kanizet visited our home many times. He was in charge of removing Onizoit's body, he also followed the later actions of the Whites. Unfortunately, he could not help us directly.

"Why can't you replace Onizoit? Why don't you devour our nightmares, as he did?" Martha asked. "The matter of caring for your home falls within the remit of the Whites now. You must understand - we rarely die naturally. Citing the old laws that govern our world, the White Harpists hold back all procedures."

"And nothing can be done about it?"

Kanizet smiled at us, which did not look too attractive.

"All that needs to be done is to defeat one of their Chief Singers during the gathering at Skeleton Lake. Unfortunately, none of the Blacks is able to match them."

So it looked like our mission just got a little more concrete.

"Who are these Chief Singers actually?" I asked.

"They are the winners of many duels for words. Advancement in the Singers' hierarchy can only be achieved in one way - being the best of them all, the real Bard."

"Isn't there any Chief Singer among the Blacks? "

"Unfortunately, no one like that has appeared for many centuries. I am afraid that this is the result of a certain specialization. We deal with the neutralization of dreams, and the Whites invent them, so they are naturally a bit more creative."

In this world, Evil apparently triumphed. Or maybe I should not apply the terrestrial definitions to the local conditions?

"I mean... You know... Our only chance is to do something almost impossible?" Martha concluded.

"It's not that bad, I can give you a hint," replied the Neanderthal.

He had a fairly well-developed strategy to fight the White Singers, but - as he himself admitted - he lacked big caliber weapons. Well, in his opinion, the leaders of the opposition party were well-read and were perfectly familiar with pop culture, but luckily, there were several gaps in their knowledge. None of the Whites knew fantasy literature very well, even though the hard science fiction was one of their strongest points. Song lyrics could also prove to be a good shot, although in this case there was a slightly greater risk of failure. Alfred wanted to know what the prospects looked like in terms of classical literature, but Kanizet did not have good information for him.

"They have mastered the so-called canon, especially one of them," he said.

"So," I turned to Alfred. "How is your Pratchett and Martin?"

"There shouldn't be any problems, although I am a bit afraid that the Discworld and Game of Thrones also belong to the canon."

We not only needed a good insight into book quotes. We had to count on the proverbial luck.

***

The greatest advantage of the Land of Dreams was the lack of dreams. We did not feel tired, so there was no need to fall asleep. We were going in the direction of the mountains, which grew in our eyes with each step, sometimes summoning us with white snow tops, and sometimes disappearing in a shroud of mists. There was something ghastly but also solemn in our journey. As if we were following not illusions, but at least some alternative path of spirituality. A journey is not only moving from place to place - it also involves the osmotic absorption of the landscapes you pass, the penetration of two models of reality: the internal and the external, leaving your traces in the sand. Each trip is a rite of passage.

The Skeleton Lake was getting closer, so we threw various quotes as part of the preparations for the skirmish with the Whites' Chief

Singers. The land from the fairytale resounded with the words of Philip Pullman and Zofia Kossak-Szczucka, I confessed love to Martha, using Tom Waits, Donna Tartt and Muniek Staszczyk, and Alfred chased away the clouds, repeating the words of Kate Bush and Kurt Vonnegut. Sometimes we lacked adequate riposte, and then we applied more general metaphors drawn from Dubrovnik court poetry. Our confidence increased with each hour, only Kanizet, leading us along the shortest route to the place, shook his head with dissatisfaction. He claimed that it would take a miracle for us to beat the White Harpists' Singers. But after all, we were in the Land of Miracles, weren't we? And so we marched and talked, waving the airy cobwebs of dreams in the wind, while believing that nothing could surprise us. We were very naive.

Chapter 22

ALFRED

The Skeleton Lake did not really have much in common with its sinister name. It evoked strong associations with our Morskie Oko, although there was a completely flat are: ne side. It was there that countless tents, yurts and pavilions were put up, and hundreds of multicolored ropes were stretched among them, with peacock feathers, light balls and a whole lot of other decorations spun into them. These decorations constituted an open and gaudy contrast to the clothes of the characters gathered in this tent town. They were dominated by, surprise, surprise, black and white robes.

Only now I noticed a rather strange circumstance. All three of us - Martha, Marc and I - were dressed (if you can use this term here) in red. Was there any color symbolism behind it, the hidden meaning of the message, or a dream interpretation? I did not have a clue.

We got to the campsite from the side of the grassy plateau, so we had the lake on the right. The inhabitants of this settlement seemed to ignore our presence, or maybe the sight of strangers simply was not unusual here. We were heading to the largest of the pavilions, in which, as Kanizet insisted, the Main Singers were staying.

"Do you feel, I don't know, the unreality of this place?" Martha asked.

"Oh, no, you are wrong," said our black guide. "Mal Valamares is the most real area in all worlds. Here is the source of all the music, which is the soundtrack of your life."

"Mal Valamares? Is this how this place is called?" Marc made sure.

"This name was written down in the oldest chronicles," Kanizet nodded.

"I still can't understand one thing," Martha said. "You're talking about a soundtrack, and I'm still thinking about something. Well, what do the dreams and music have in common with each other?"

"The oldest musical instruments were created on Earth about thirty-five thousand years ago," I added. "Even Oliver Sacks wrote about it. Wagner was struggling with the orchestra introduction to the Das Rheingold, and finally the solution came in a strange, half-hallucinatory state. Ravel noted that the most wonderful melodies came to him in a dream, as it was with Stravinsky. In fact, many of the great classical composers mentioned musical dreams in which they often found important inspiration. They were, among others, Haendel, Mozart, Chopin or Brahms."

"You are absolutely right," Added Kanizet. "And coming back to your question, Martha... Dreams must have some real element in them, some warp around which our imagination is weaving. Music is such an element of real life. Someone even said that music is our only power not changed by a dream, while actions, character, visual elements and language undergo significant changes."

"Can we use it somehow?" Marc was interested.

"I am afraid that in terms of musical skills, we are slightly inferior - Black Harpist had bad news."

But we finally arrived at the big white pavilion on the bank of the lake. I wondered what formalities had to be met so that we could face the Chief Singers. However, it was not too difficult. It seemed that the guards already knew about our presence, because they left us a free way, doubling in bows.

Our antagonists were standing on a platform. There were two of them - one short, quite portly, and the other as if his opposite - tall and athletically built. Even the white robes hanging on their bodies could not hide the asymmetry of their silhouettes. The whole was complemented by the obligatory masks and relatively long, braided hair. The braids were white, in case anybody wondered.

The taller one approached us at a distance of few meters and asked:

"Do thee know the discourse ritual, is not it, or is it so?"

Then I noticed that Martha and Marc were beginning to stare at him, as if his voice had evoked a memory of something. The second of the Singers also stepped forward and repeated the question spoken by his companion.

Marc hissed in surprise.

"Show your faces immediately! What the hell is going on?" He shouted.

Both masked men seemed slightly baffled. After a moment, however, with some reluctance, they took off the elements of the costume. Their old faces, plowed with wrinkles, had a difficult to define passion. Martha just shouted.

"It's these policemen! Sabol and Śmigielski!"

As far as I remember, they were the investigating officers, repeatedly calling my friends for interrogation, or harassing them in their own home. Knowledge on this subject in no way explained their presence or appearance though.

"The police employ such old people? I thought one retires in the forties there?" I asked rather suspiciously.

"It's them, but they have changed, as if something had aged them several dozen years." Marc replied quickly.

"Let us reveal some details for you," the lower of the two old men said.

"Yes, you'll do it best, no?" Added the other.

"I can't wait, AC Śmigielski," said Martha.

"No one has called me that for a long tim," the Harpist smiled and began his story.

It turned out that they both got here thanks to a certain drug many years ago. According to Śmigielski, the side effect of taking this substance was a time travel. Sabol had, as it turned out, a different theory on this subject.

"We are in the realm of dreams. Here, all cause-and-effect relations disappear, everything is mixed up. Here the cause may be later than the effect," he maintained.

I remembered that I had felt asleep only a dozen or so seconds before the Majewski family, and yet they arrived here many hours after me.

"It doesn't matter," Marc said. "If you are you, the matter is settled. Assign us a Black Harpist and we can go home."

Śmigielski looked at Sabol.

"I'm afraid it will not be that easy," he said to us with an apologetic smile.

"Why is that?" Martha was surprised.

Sabol looked at us for a long time.

"Because it was us who killed, no, the guardian of your dreams."

Chapter 23

MARC

We were flabbergasted. There was no sense in what Sabol said, no logic, the rational thinking failed completely. Suddenly, Alfred began to laugh.

"   ,   haven't I thought about it! It's elementary!" Apparently he could not stop laughing.

"Ehm... Can you kindly enlighten us?" My wife interrupted him.

"Of course. Listen. Well, these two have traveled into the past and have made a good career here since then. However, in order to be able to get here at all, they had to initiate a cause-and-effect sequence. It all started with this corpse in your home, right? So they waited for the right moment - they had to coordinate it perfectly in the time line - and they slayed poor Onizoit in cold blood. Thanks to that, they have appeared in this story."

The former policemen listened with sour faces.

"Almost everything is right, congratulations on your deduction," Śmigielski drawled. "Now you understand why everything must remain as it is. Why you have to wake up from this dream, before slowly slipping into the madness of the dream nightmares."

"To tell you the truth, I don't understand," Alfred pointed out. "It would not cost you anything."

"You are very wrong," replied Sabol. "We are the stars of the stage here, the kings, celebrities and actors in one. You want us to renounce it, no?"

"But you can stay here while we will return to normality," I noticed.

"You don't understand the entirety of the whole thing," Śmigielski shook his head. "We both operate here a little bit on the principle of anomaly, precisely because the balance between the Whites and the Blacks was disturbed..."

"You have disturbed this balance yourself," I clarified.

"It's irrelevant now. We must eliminate you. That's why I will ask you again, do thee know the ritual of discourse, is it not, or is it so?"

There was silence. Alfred broke it.

"We know, and note the fact that you never have a second opportunity to make the first impression."*

The blow was strong and came almost without a warning. Śmigielski, however, smiled crookedly and replied:

"You confuse the sky with the stars, reflected at night on the surface of the pond."

I guess they were not as lousy at fantasy as we thought. The former policeman confirmed this immediately, using Sapkowski again.

"Soon, there won't be any vampires, wyverns, endriagas or werewolves in the world. But there will always be motherfuckers!"

Alfred bent under the weight of this sentence, under its timeless accuracy. It was time for a slight change in the repertoire.

"In our lifetime, we carry mountains in our bones. We turn into them after death." This quotation was rather a paraphrase, because it looked a bit different in the original.

---

* Perhaps the readers would prefer to guess the source of the quotes for themselves. But the provisions of the copyright law are inexorable, so I have to say that the books mentioned are: Sword of Destiny, Time of Contempt and Lady of the Lake by Andrzej Sapkowski, Shadows Linger by Glen Cook, Lies of Locke Lamora by Scott Lynch, and the series about Ferrina by Katarzyna Michalak. [author's note]

Śmigielski frowned. I could clearly see that he was searching his memory for a suitable retort. In the Main Hall of the pavilion, everyone was standing like white statues, listening to the exchange of arguments.

"Fortune is an unstable whore, crazy about irony," finally said the shorter Singer.

My friend apparently took this sentence as a desperate attempt of a defense. So he attacked with Scott Lynch.

"Someday, you're going to fuck up so magnificently, so ambitiously, so overwhelmingly, that the sky will light up and the moons will spin and the gods themselves will shit comets with glee," he drawled triumphantly.

Śmigielski's face was transparent for a moment.

"Every dream, the enchanting one and the beautiful one, when dreamed for too long, turns into a nightmare. And from this we wake up screaming!" He ended with a strong emphasis.

I must admit that the quote was very well chosen. I began to worry about our fate, but then I noticed Alfred's satanic smile.

"The licks of hundreds of tongues on the hands, wounded during teleportation!" He shouted.

I could not recognize this book at all. The White Singers seemed to be equally surprised. And that was just the beginning. Alfred quickly made another statement.

"The wind wailed in the dark, carrying with it a scent that could change the fate of the world!"

The figures of the policemen began to blur in the light of gas lamps that hang in the corners of the hall. And then the librarian brought the final feint.

"On the path, where just a moment ago there was nothing, or at least nothing remarkable, stood a tall man of unusual, simply unearthly beauty..."

The silhouettes of Sabol and Śmigielski trembled like the candle flames for a moment, and then - as if someone blew those flames - they disappeared. At that moment, two more people emerged from the group of the figures in white robes.

"We hereby acknowledge the sending of our brothers to the whiter White. Thus, we appoint a new guardian of dreams who will take the position of the Black killed in the battlefield."

It looked like we were saved. One thing still bothered me though.

"Listen, Alfred. Where were these last quotes with which you defeated them from?"

My friend looked at me for a long time.

"You don't want to know that. Believe me, you don't."

EPILOGUE

Majewski woke up first. The dreams were still buzzing in their heads, and they could still feel the breeze of the wind, tugging the tents at the Skeleton Lake, on their faces. Marc stood up, stretched slightly.

"I'm going to see what Alfred is doing, honey..."

"Go, go. We've succeeded, right? Do you feel that this nightmare is over?" Martha smiled.

"Yes, I have the impression that someone has taken a huge burden off my chest."

He went toward the living room, turned to his wife again, made an intimate gesture, and then stood in the door. He left the room, then returned to bed with a very strange expression.

"We have to call the police. Alfred is dead."

"What?"

"Do you remember the ending of our dream?" Marc asked.

"Not exactly."

"He stayed there, Martha. He will be a Singer."

"I don't believe that! He is our friend! We need to do something!"

Marc shrugged.

"It's probably the price for our mental health."

They both went into the living room. Alfred was lying on the couch with a look of surprise on his face. His open eyes stared at the wall, as if they were seeing more than just an old-fashioned wallpaper pattern. As if they were looking somewhere inside. And a blue dawn was waking up outside the window, because the first snow of this year fell this night. "The corpses must be viewed in blue light, it brings out the most beautiful side of them," Martha thought.

THE END

ACKNOWLEDGEMENTS

This novel was being created for several years, so it is not unexpected that I have incurred a lot of gratitude debt during this time. I will try to repay it now.

Thank you to all the readers, who have been waiting patiently, asking every now and then: "when will you finally finish this novel?" Here it is, my dear - it stands among the shadows on your shelf, grinning and waiting for a convenient moment to jump.

Thank you, Sebastian Sokołowski, for believing in me. You know, Seba, that writing horror literature in Poland is a niche activity. And writing ambitious horror literature that tries to be something more, is a niche within a niche. I keep my fingers crossed for all your promotional and publishing activities - and I don't mean only my book, but the works of other creators who are and will be published by you.

Thank you, Anna Musiałowicz - the editor of Dreaming Walls. The writer does not know what terrible mistakes he makes until he meets a real editor.

I thank everyone who read the initial version of the book and shared their insightful remarks with me - I am writing about you here, Agnieszka Kwiatkowska, Monika Śniedziewska-Lerczak, Magdalena Bułka and Błażej Jaworski. Thanks!

Special thanks also to Kazimierz Kyrcz Jr. - he did not read the manuscript, but he shared with me a lot of information about the work of the Police and the police hierarchy. Kazek - I will always remember that you noticed my story in "Fantastic Magazine" a long time ago, and your support convinced me to involve more in writing.

I thank my children - Hania and Filip, to whom I owe about seventy percent of the lines of the children in the Dreaming Walls. You are my inspiration and one of the reasons I live for.

First of all, however, I would like to thank my wife, Magdalena. Only You know how hard it is to live under one roof with a writer tormented by demons. Thanks to You, I want to fight these demons. You have supported me at every step over the years, You read everything I wrote and gave me courage. There is nothing without You.